LETTERS T

# MATCHED my

# CHRISTMAS

## Crush

**A SWEET OFF-LIMITS
HOLIDAY ROMCOM**

# FRANCESCA SPENCER

This one is for you, Kate W, my wonderful, kindhearted, talented friend.

# Matched With My Christmas Crush

**A** classroom teacher. A swoony single dad. Undeniable tingles spark at *The Christmas Spectacular.*

### *James*

Santa's helper at this year's community Christmas show? My son, Alfie.

The unexpected bonus to Alfie's theatrical debut? Seeing his teacher, Miss Flo Simmons, at rehearsals.

When she's around, I light up like a Christmas tree.

It could just be the effects of tinsel and glitter but I'm feeling something I thought was lost.

Flo, however, is strictly off-limits. Even if I wanted to date again, my priority is being Alfie's dad.

### *Flo*

It's possibly the holly-jolly time of year, but James Hadley, the attractive dad of one of my students, is turning my insides to Jello.

On the stage, we get stuck behind a plywood snowman. Close together in the dark, my pulse races when we almost kiss.

But romance is a no-no. This fluttery crush won't last.

Like melting snow, it'll be gone, unless some mistletoe magic happens.

***Matched With My Christmas Crush**, an off-limits novella, is book 11 of the **Letters to Mrs. Claus** multi-author series—a kisses-only romantic comedy col-*

*lection bursting with holiday cheer. Each story is linked through Mrs. Claus's Operation Mistletoe Match, where she receives a letter from a meddling friend or family member about someone lonely, heartbroken, or closed off to love. With her timeless wisdom, Mrs. Claus pens a tailored message to the subject of the letter, offering an inspiring note that tackles their romantic roadblock. Packed with hilarious mishaps, flustered blushes, and courageous adventures as they chase their happily-ever-after in this no-spice, swoon-worthy series!*

# Prologue

I t's that time of year again—the holiday season! The air practically sparkles, and the smell of baking ginger-bread makes even frosty days feel cozy. Here at the North Pole, we are reminded of what this season brings most of all— the gentle glow of joy and love that wraps around every heart.

Take this letter, for instance:

Dear Mrs. Claus,

I hope you are well.
I am Alfie. My dad is James. My mom passt away. I don't rember her. I was to young. I am older now. My dad is very old. He works a lot. He says he is fine. But sometimes he is sad. I think he wants a girl-frend.

Please please please help my dad get a girl-frend.

I know some1 prity he likes a lot. Miss S. (I can't tel you her name. It's a seecret. BIG CLUe - I see her evry day at school!!!)
I am in the Christmas show. Santa's Cheef Elf!!! The show is called The Christmas Spectacular.
Spectacular = ORSUM. I get to sing a song and fly in the slaye with Santa. (We don't realy fly. And it's not realy Santa. Haha.)

My dad and Miss S help on the show. My dad larfs a lot.
I hope you can make my wish come ture and make my dad hapy.
Thank U and Mery Christmas!
Lots of luv,
xxx Alfie Hadley

Dear Mrs. Claus,

I hope you are well. I am Alfie. My dad is James. My mom passed away. I don't remember her. I was too young. I am older now. My dad is very old. He works a lot. He says he is fine. But sometimes he is sad. I think he wants a girlfriend.

**Please please please** help my dad get a girlfriend.

I know someone pretty he likes a lot. **Miss S**. (I can't tell you her name. It's a secret. **BIG CLUE** - I see her every day at school!!!)

I am in the Christmas show. Santa's Cheif Elf!!! The show is called The Christmas Spectacular. Spectacular = AWESOME. I get to sing a song and fly in the sleigh with Santa. (We don't really fly. And it's not really Santa. Haha.) My dad and Miss S help on the show. My dad laughs a lot. I hope you can make my wish come true and make my dad happy.

Thank you and Merry Christmas!
Lots of love,
x x x Alfie Hadley

Sounds like Alfie Hadley needs some help. He is hoping his dad will open his heart again and let love in. A tall order, perhaps, but nothing a little Christmas miracle can't handle.

Who am I to meddle in matters of the heart, you wonder?

Why, I'm Mrs. Claus, and I'm more than just the cookie-baker of the North Pole. While my dear Santa and his elves bustle about with toys and tinsel, ensuring Christmas morning sparkles for children everywhere, I have my own mission: *Operation Mistletoe Match*.

Through these letters, I weave a bit of hope, a whisper to take a chance—because love is the greatest gift, and it's waiting to be unwrapped.

The story on the following pages is of Flo and James. Did my letter spark the courage they needed? That's for you to discover.

So, hang a 'Do Not Disturb' sign on the door, settle into your favorite chair, and enjoy this story that's waiting just for you.

With mistletoe kisses and a heart full of hope,
*Mrs. Claus*

# Chapter One

## FLO

Rehearsals for *The Christmas Spectacular,* an all-singing, all-dancing, multi-generational community event, have taken over the Woodhill Community Center's workshop and hall. There is, I'm told, a loose narrative around a Christmas fairy and a lonely snowman that links the scenes of songs and high-kicking chorus lines.

Our ambitious director, Lester Herman, believes in good ol' fashioned family entertainment with all the razzmatazz of Broadway in the fifties.

"We might be performing on a small-town stage, but our hearts are in the stars, and our souls are made for the bright lights of Hollywood, darlings!" Or something like that.

There are other performances in the community theater calendar, but the Christmas show is the highlight of the year. Everyone is either in it or knows someone in it. When the Christmas production is in full swing, cue the lights, music, and action of fun festive tingles. I love getting involved in the madness at this crazy time of year.

Briana, my friend from school, is already here at the workshop/rehearsal space with her husband, Tony. Their two girls are dancers, performing as fairies in Act One, mice in Act Two, and gingerbread people in Act Three. Tony is a driving force behind the Woodhill Community Theater. He is the foreman of the construction crew and has a big heart to match his big voice.

"Hey, Flo," he booms when I walk in. "You made it."

Briana waves and comes over to greet me. "There's so much to do. It's all hands on deck. Come and help me glitter the Christmas trees and stockings," she says, handing me a gluey brush.

Briana and I carefully lay out the pieces of brightly painted scenery, apply glue in artistic daubs, then sprinkle silver and gold glitter onto the wet glue - the finishing touch that instantly adds a Christmasy shimmer.

"Looking good," says Tony, walking over to us. Someone else is with him, but I'm bending over, intent on glittering and not paying attention. "This is James."

"Hi." I straighten up, slightly blinded by glitter. "James?" I ask, trying to focus, as it dawns on me who Tony is introducing. "Mr. Hadley? Alfie's dad?"

"That's right," James says, holding out a hand for me to shake, but my fingers are covered in glue and glitter, so I just wave. "Miss Simmons?"

"Call me Flo. I'm only Miss Simmons in class."

"Flo. Great." James smiles warmly. "I know we've only met a couple of times at school, but I feel as if I know all about you. Alfie tells me every day about how much he likes you." James glances at the floor, then shyly says, "He's quite a fan, in case you didn't know."

Hearing this makes me blush. Alfie Hadley is one of the most endearing yet challenging kids in my class. We're not supposed to have favorites, but he is absolutely adorable. I just want to hug him. Or strangle him. One or the other. Alfie has a great imagination, but has difficulty following instructions sometimes. He's often in his own little world and needs constant reminders about staying on task.

For example, in a math lesson about grouping fives and tens, he made me a paper flower from a page torn from his exercise book. How do I deal with something like that? Adorable.

I'm blushing, of course, because James Hadley is one of the most handsome men I've ever seen. He's accidentally handsome; casually handsome. I'm not saying that he doesn't care about his appearance, but he just looks effortlessly good. Even in his worn-out coveralls, he looks good.

Our eyes meet. Feeling self-conscious, I look away and concentrate on gluing and glittering. But I can't help watching out of the corner of my eye, as he sweeps clean, manicured fingers through his dark, wavy hair. My heart softens like a chocolate yule log in front of a roaring fire. I wonder if he knows the effect he has on me.

I first met James Hadley when he walked into my classroom - thus unintentionally scrambling my sensible life - at the beginning of the school year. It was a standard 'Meet the Teacher' evening. I had my usual presentation all cued up and ready to go, but my mind went blank when he shook my hand. His touch instantly turned me into a bumbling idiot, and I forgot what I had prepared. I don't actually remember what I said. Probably a string of nonsense. In a nanosecond, the allotted ten-minute slot with James Hadley ended, and I said goodbye to the most gorgeous single dad in the whole wide world all too soon. But no time for mushy thoughts. I quickly pulled myself together because the next set of parents was waiting for me in the corridor.

Since meeting Mr. *Dreamy* Hadley, I've found it hard to concentrate on grading papers. Or anything. Was it his soft brown eyes that interrupted my lesson planning? Or his cool politeness, bordering on arrogance, that I couldn't shake off when I should have been working on assessments? James Hadley is at once charming but shy; open yet distant. His smile conveys warmth, inviting you closer, and yet warns you to stay away. In ten minutes – no, more like ten seconds - James Hadley had turned my insides to Jello and my brain to sticky toffee pudding. With cream.

I remember, after that 'Meet the Teacher' evening, when the last set of parents finally left, I rushed into Briana's classroom, breathlessly leaning my back against the closed door. I told her that I'd just met the most infuriating man who had turned me into a babbling fool.

"Is he that handsome?"

"Who said anything about handsome?" I pace up and down Briana's classroom. "I just said that he was infuriating."

"I'm getting Mr. Darcy vibes." Briana leans across her desk with fingers interlaced like a medical doctor.

I stop pacing and stare at my friend. "Bri, James Hadley is the most infuriatingly handsome man I have ever met in my whole life."

"He sounds perfect," Briana says, flashing a sideways smile at me.

I collapse on a child-sized chair, swooning in the style of a pre-Raphaelite heroine, and tell her that she's right. He is perfect, but nothing romantic could ever happen because Mr. James *Dreamy* Hadley is the dad of one of my students.

"Oh, dear," Briana says, looking up from her laptop screen. "That does make things awkward." She takes off her glasses and relaxes back in her adult-sized chair. "But not impossible."

That was at the start of the school year. Since then, the memory of James has wafted in and out of my daydreams at random, inappropriate moments. His handsome face drifts across my unconscious and distracts me from being a practical, systematic, organized elementary school teacher.

Now it's close to Christmas, and here he is again. My heart is doing somersaults. My stomach is doing flips. My brain has disconnected from my mouth. I can't form words.

Tony slaps James on the back. "Enough chitchat. James, can you work with Flo? I need Briana, my love, to please help with Santa's sleigh."

Thrown totally off balance, I gulp, and I'm about to scurry after my friend, but Briana shoots me one of her stern teacher glares. I freeze where I am. It works on her class of eight-year-olds, and it works on me.

I give myself a virtual slap. 'Just be cool,' I tell myself. Then, picking up a gluey brush, I hand it to James, and effortlessly, casually say, "Is this your first time glittering a stage set, or are you a trained professional?"

"I'm brand new to this," James says, smiling. He dips his brush in the glue. "I think I may need your expert guidance, Flo."

It takes about three seconds to go over the rudiments of glittering. Then James suggests that he does the gluing while I follow with the glitter, which seems like a good plan. We settle into a gluey-glitter rhythm. I relax a little and ask what brings him to a grubby, draughty community hall on a Friday night.

"Alfie is a naughty elf."

"That's right. He is," I say, remembering the time when Alfie made a Jenga-style tower out of Cuisenaire rods in a literacy lesson. "Oh, you mean in the show?"

"Yes. I know. Perfect casting, huh?" James laughs. "Alfie is so proud to get a main part and is so excited about performing; he sort of talked me into volunteering." James blobs some glue. "He can be very persuasive, you know."

"Yes. I do know."

"Said that if he was in the show, then I should be too. I can't argue with that kind of logic." I melt to mush as I listen and forget to glitter. James reminds me. Then he says, "But there was no way I was going to get up there and perform in front of people. So, helping out on the set and backstage is the compromise we came to." We glue and glitter some more. "I suppose I'm a bit bah-humbug about Christmas, if left to my own devices." James pauses for a moment. "Christmas is all about kids, isn't it?"

"Oh, I don't think that's the case. But children give adults a good excuse to get festive and glittery."

"Yes. You're right about that." James looks at his gluey and glittery hands, then he asks, "And what about you? How come you're here?"

"Ah, I'm here for... Why am I here?" I look around at the other volunteers busily finishing pieces of the stage set. "Volunteering is good fun. And *The Christmas Spectacular* would not be possible without a solid community commitment." I liberally scatter gold and silver sparkles. "There's a joyful madness in staging a two-and-a-half-hour show. If you add up the insane number of man-hours in logistics, construction, and rehearsals; the cost of materials, power, and space rental; calculate the sheer effort, enthusiasm, and passion that goes into a show like this one, it doesn't make any kind of sense on a spreadsheet. It's bonkers. But all this," I wave an arm in a wide arc, "... is not really about putting on a show. I didn't fully understand, until I got involved, that the real purpose of all this craziness is bringing the community together." I stop talking because I'm aware that what I'm saying has turned into a rant. I look away, then say with a grin, "It's going to be fantastic!"

Tony calls everyone to attention. "Lester is just about ready for the Christmas trees; the giant snowflakes; and the fireplace," he says, reading from his clipboard. "Which means we can finish up the sleigh; the snowy hills; and Rapunzel's tower for the next half hour, then we'll switch them over." He looks up. "Any questions?" He waits for a second, then says, "Good. Let's make this happen!"

"So, according to the script," James says, as we carry pieces of scenery to the main hall for the walk-through. "Santa and Alfie are going to fly down onto the stage in that sleigh." He nods at a plywood cutout.

"Sounds technical and possibly hazardous," I say, mildly concerned.

"Well, I've been assured that relevant health and safety measures are up to date and in place. The sleigh will be attached to a crane and not reliant on pixie dust or a decent level of Christmas spirit in the audience for flight." We set the pieces down where directed. "Lester says the sleigh scene will be the highlight of the entire show. Alfie's buzzed about it."

As if by magic, Alfie appears at my elbow, followed by Mrs. Edna Appleby, who runs the after-school program and is universally recognized as a national treasure. James hugs his son, and I greet Mrs. Appleby. Everyone calls her Mrs. Appleby.

"Hey, Dad. Hey, Miss Simmons," Alfie says with a big grin.

"Hey, Bud." James tousles his son's hair. "How was school today?" James flashes a dazzling smile my way. His smile and the gentle way he interacts with his little boy throw me off-balance again. Alfie shoots me a worried look, making me laugh.

"Was it that bad, Alfie?" I say with mock concern, which seems to put Santa's elf at ease.

"I'm almost done here, Bud," James says. "Then I'm coming to watch, okay?" Alfie looks up, nodding vigorously, then he wraps his arms around his dad.

"Wow!" Lester enters with arms outstretched. "The sleigh is going to look Ay-mazing, guys. It's a shame we won't be using real live reindeer, but cutouts will have to do." He claps his hands together. "Come on, everyone.

Take your places for The Grand Finale. Alfie. I hope you've
learned your words."

# *Chapter Two*

## JAMES

### A few weeks later

"Alfie! Hurry up. We're going to be late for Mrs. Appleby," I yell up the stairs, accompanied by a series of thumps as Alfie stampedes overhead. So much noise for such a small boy.

I put Alfie's Spiderman lunchbox in his backpack and discover a half-wrapped, half-eaten cheese sandwich from the day before. Not unusual. I groan out loud as I retrieve the squishy discarded morsel and, leaving the backpack on the floor, I run to the kitchen to dispose of it in the trash. Aware of time ticking away, I quickly return to the hall, patting down my pockets, checking for phone, keys, and wallet. Then I grab our coats from the unruly bundle on hooks by the door. Mornings are always a rush, but today, all progress toward leaving seems to be hampered at every turn.

"Now, Alfie!" I yell, reaching for my son's backpack, but I pause when I spot an envelope on the floor. I don't recall seeing it earlier. It may have just arrived in the minute when I was dealing with Alfie's half-eaten lunch. Hooking the backpack over my shoulder, I pick up the intriguing envelope and slowly turn it over. It's addressed to me. Probably some promotional or advertising material. I check my watch. I don't have time to open it now. It can wait. I'm anticipating a wall-to-wall workload when I get to the office. I should have set the alarm earlier, but here we are, running late. Again.

Finally, Alfie charges down the stairs, undone shoelaces trailing like an accident waiting to happen. "What did I tell you about tying your laces, Alf?" I say, exasperated. "You'll trip and fall."

"I thought we were late," says Alfie, bending to tie his shoes, "… and needed to leave right away."

There's no time for this kind of discussion. I shove the envelope in my pocket and usher my chaotic son out of the house. We march together next door, up the path, where Mrs. Appleby is waiting for us. I hand Alfie his backpack while apologizing profusely.

"Oh, don't worry, James," Mrs. Appleby says, smiling broadly. She has a way of calming a situation as if she has everything under control, which she does.

Sighing with gratitude, I instantly relax and say with hand on heart, "I don't know what I would do without you, Edna. Sincerely." Then, I turn to Alfie, give him a quick squeeze, and tousle his hair. "Bye, Son. Be good. I'll see you later."

My day, as expected, is foot-to-the-floor busy. With only a few workdays left on the calendar, the countdown to Christmas and the holidays, everyone wants a tidy end-of-year wrap-up. And finalized projections for the New Year's quarter. On days such as these, I reconsider my commitment to volunteering on *The Christmas Spectacular* and anything else that eats into my already stretched schedule.

I'm out of my comfort zone at the community theater. Doing anything involving paint and glitter is alien and not a sensible, productive use of my time that I usually charge out in fifteen-minute slots. I'm used to spreadsheets, tidy columns, reporting with data, and making numbers add up. Messy theater is the opposite of being a business consultant.

However, these brief moments of regret are swept away and replaced with proud memories of my son at rehearsals, on stage, singing his heart out, and being the best Santa's helper in the history of community theater Christmas productions.

I didn't anticipate how much Alfie's confidence would grow and shine in his starring role. I am so happy to witness his progress, to be right there supporting him, from his timid audition, when he could hardly squeak his lines, to belting out the showstopping finale at the front of the stage and the entire cast. Sure, I would have seen the show on performance night. Up in the front row, cheering my kid. But the experience of us both being involved in the show has been really special and has brought us closer together.

Also, volunteering on the Christmas show has been the perfect low-key opportunity to get to know Miss Flo Simmons. Sharing time with Alfie's teacher was such an unexpected gift.

When we first met at Alfie's school at the start of term, she took my breath away. I was tongue-tied when she welcomed me into the classroom and showed me Alfie's table and some of his artwork on display. I felt shy. Awkward. I forgot to ask pertinent questions about my son's education. The allotted ten minutes ended too soon.

"Thanks for coming this evening," Flo said as she showed me out of the classroom. "Children thrive when parents are actively involved in their learning. Alfie is lucky to have you."

I don't know what she thought about me, but I thought she was lovely. It's been a while since I noticed a pretty woman. I don't date. I'm out of practice romantically. But there's nothing the least bit romantic about me and Flo. There can't be. The crystal-clear boundaries of parents and teachers are set in stone. We can be friends. We can hang out. Platonically. There's a respectful line that can never be crossed, and that's fine with me.

Then again, there's something utterly captivating about Flo that occupies my mind. The way she laughs. The way her eyes sparkle. She is right there in my thoughts when I'm not even thinking of anything. Some random memory will pop into my head that triggers a smile. Something she said to make me laugh, perhaps, or a memory of us – dusty; both wearing coveralls; shifting scenery; putting props in place; getting *The Christmas Spectacular* ready for performance night.

Since Alfie's mother passed away when he was still a baby, I've been protecting my world. I'm a private, self-reliant, independent person. I thought that Alfie and I would be better off by ourselves. Just him and me: high-fiving, hanging out, playing ball, and having a great time. Father and son. And we were, for a while.

Then we both got to know Flo outside of school. She is a delight. We clicked right away and always seemed to be together, working on the stage set, helping out. Sure, we were with others from the theater crowd, but the three of us bonded. After rehearsals, sometimes, we'd go out for something to eat. We had a great time. Hanging out, chatting, and laughing. I'd say we were the happiest people around.

I wonder if, after the Christmas show finishes, we could stay friends, or would that be weird? However, the more time we spend together, the more the parent–teacher lines seem to be blurring.

There have been a few times recently, where our hands have accidentally touched, or she has looked into my eyes, and it felt as if she sensed, like me, that there was something more between us.

In these moments, people, noise, and everything else in the room melt away. Time stands still. It feels wonderful. A kind of blissful contentment washes over me. A truth. An absolute. Pure clarity. I want to reach out to hold Flo's hand - not accidentally but intentionally - and be beside her forever.

But maybe I'm just imagining the spark of attraction between us. Maybe the magic of being with Flo is fleeting, like the echo of applause dying out when the show ends. Maybe we're only friends because we're volunteering on the Christmas production, and that is the only glue of common ground holding us together. I don't want to live in hope of something that will never be. And I have my son to consider. It's not fair to Alfie if I get too close to anyone. For the moment, anyway. Maybe when he's older, I'll think about dating, but there's no rush, is there?

I realize that I've been staring at my monitor, doing nothing. The cursor blinks back at me from the screen. It's almost time to pick up Alfie from Mrs. Appleby's.

As I pack up my things, I remember the envelope from this morning is still unopened in my pocket. I pat down the outside of my jacket, making the paper crinkle pleasantly. In the car, I take out the envelope, read the front, then I turn it over to read the sender's name – Mrs. Claus, *Operation Mistletoe Match.*

A joke, I imagine, from someone in the neighborhood. Mrs. Appleby, probably. I smile to myself as I start the engine. One cute joke. Sooner or later, I'll find out who the sender posing as the legendary Mrs. Claus really is, and we'll have a good laugh about it.

A few names pop into my head. Mrs. Appleby is top of the list. But then, it could be Flo's teaching friend, Briana. Or possibly Tony? No. Tony wouldn't go to such lengths to make a point. I ponder my list of letter-sending conspirators on the drive home and conclude, with almost one hundred percent certainty, that Mrs. Appleby is behind the mysterious sweet-smelling mail.

Reaching my neighbor's house, I ring the doorbell and prepare to confront Mrs. Appleby with the very cute joke envelope. While I wait outside, I hear Alfie say something to her. She says something back, and they both laugh. Soon, I hear footsteps, and Edna Appleby opens the door.

"Ah, Mrs. Appleby," I begin. "You have such a great sense of humor."

My neighbor smiles at me as if I'm the one who is playing a prank. "James. You're in a very good mood. And, yes, you're right. I am blessed with a great sense of humor."

Alfie pushes past and wraps his arms around my waist. "Hey, Dad," he says.

"Hey, Son." I hug him right back. "Are you ready to go? Where's your bag? What about your jacket? Go get your things. Lace up your shoes."

I watch Alfie scamper away down the hall, then I hold out the letter to show Mrs. Appleby. "Then, you'll admit that this is your handiwork?"

Mrs. Appleby takes the letter from me and holds it up close to her face. She sniffs the paper and says, "Mmmm, gingerbread." She smiles, her eyes twinkle. "I'd say that this letter is from Mrs. Claus." I'm about to counter her assumption, but she continues, cutting me off. "Mrs. Claus and Operation Mistletoe Match are pretty good at giving people the nudge they need to find true love."

"But it's not real, is it? She, I mean. Mrs. Claus..."

"Oh, I'd say she is very real," says Mrs. Appleby. Her tone is surprisingly serious. "About as real as the letter you're holding in your hand."

"So, you're telling me that you didn't send the letter?"

"That's right, James. No. It wasn't me," Mrs. Appleby says, still twinkling. "But maybe it should have been."

I put the letter back in my pocket as Alfie scoots out, his jacket flapping open, swinging his backpack. "Ready, Dad!" he yells.

# Chapter Three

# FLO

Christmas fizz is everywhere as we count down the days, like opening windows on an advent calendar, to performance night of *The Christmas Spectacular*. Our little town is charged with an electrical atmosphere that's almost tangible. People stop in the main street, say hi, and then enthuse about how this year's production is going to be The Best Ever.

In the final week of rehearsals, everything show-related is shifted from the workshop at the community hall to the theater, where tonight, fingers crossed, it all works without a hitch, on the actual stage. I feel a glow of pride as I look around at all the painted and glittery scenery and props ready for a night of sparkly theatrical magic. I know in my heart that all the effort, late nights, and drama are so worthwhile. It has been an amazing experience, working crazy long hours to pull it all together. Combustible excitement fills the frosty air. Tonight is the night. It's showtime.

Apart from pride in a job well done, one of the unexpected perks of volunteering on the Christmas show this year was sharing time with the gorgeous James Hadley. Since meeting at the start of the school year, he has been on my mind. I'm a little ashamed to admit that what I believed to be arrogance at our first meeting was merely shyness. I got over my silly, jittery teen-type crush, enough to have a reasonably coherent conversation, and James and I have become close friends while volunteering on the show. Actually, my heart nags that we're more than close friends, as I feel myself falling for James. But anything romantic between us remains strictly taboo.

It's a rare and special thing when a handsome man walks into your classroom. Rare and special, yet equally annoying when that handsome man is the dad of one of your students. Accepted professional boundaries regarding romance are instantly in place and need to be adhered to; lines that can't be crossed; rules that can't be broken.

However, with each day that we spend together, our connection deepens. James and I gravitate, like north and south magnetic poles or planets in an orbit around each other. I feel his presence in a room. In a break or after rehearsals, I'd be chatting with other volunteers and performers in the green room or at a café, and somehow, James and I always end up together. Sometimes he'll smile at me from across the stage, and for a minute, it seems as if no one else is there. Just us. It's magic. I feel wonderful.

One time, during a rehearsal of Act Three, just after the gingerbread people's entrance, James and I were at the side of the stage, waiting for the cue to change the scenery, when he accidentally touched my hand. I jumped. It was like a mild electric shock, similar to a science experiment demonstrating how energy is transferred around a circuit.

"Are you alright?" James whispered close to my ear in the dark, as the gingerbread people sang 'A Holly Jolly Christmas'.

He thought that I'd hurt myself, and the look of concern in his eyes made my knees weak. I felt so foolish that I had reacted theway I did. I laughed and shrugged it off, but we were so caught up in the moment that we almost missed the line from Charlie, the fairy, which was our cue to shift the snowy hill into place. I don't think anyone noticed.

But there are no more rehearsals. No more legitimate excuses for being close to James. No more accidental touches in the dark or the thrill of his soft whisper. After tonight, who knows what will happen? Will we just go back to our roles of parent and teacher? I'm not sure if I can be professionally distant again. Could we stay friends and keep having fun – respectful, arms-length fun? The show has been the reason for us sharing this precious time together. Without it, is there anything to connect us? This idea makes my heart heavy and takes some of the shine off the glittery excitement of performance night.

James is at the theater, talking with Tony, when I arrive. Everyone has been summoned to the stage to await instruction. I wave to James, but walk over to Briana, who is telling a funny story. I pretend to be interested and laugh where appropriate, but I'm conscious of James, who flicks a glance my way.

Lester holds up his hands then slaps them together to hush everyone. "Darlings," he begins. "We. Are. Here." He holds up his arms and reaches wriggly fingers to the ceiling. "Who's excited?" He doesn't wait for a reply. He exhales audibly. "This show is not just a show." He closes his eyes. "What do I mean by that?" He walks with measured, slow steps in a circle in front of us. "I mean, ladies and gentlemen, that this is a piece of history in the making. People will talk about this show, in this little town, for years – decades – to come. And we." His voice drops to a whisper. "Us. You and me. We are going to make sure that happens." He stops pacing and faces the performers, technicians, and stage crew. "Thank you for your hard work. Your commitment. Your time. And your belief in this production. Without you, there is no show. So, let's make it fabulous!" Lester booms out into the empty auditorium.

We cheer, clap, and whistle loudly. This is it.

"Clear the stage. Cue the music. Act one. Scene one. Starting places, please." Lester leaves the stage and takes up position in the front row of the stalls.

Everyone has a job to do. The lighting and sound operators leave by the side door and go up to the control booth with a view of the stage from the back of the auditorium. The stage managers put on their headsets and arrange their dog-eared annotated scripts. The scene shifters stand by for action. The performers in the opening number limber up, and everyone else leaves the stage to wait for their cues in the dressing rooms.

Stage lights are off. The heavy red velvet stage curtain is lowered. I stand in the wings with James and wait. Soon, the theater doors will open, and the audience will start to come in.

A few manic minutes elapse as chorus line performers find their starting places, crosses of tape stuck to the black floor of the stage. Excitement builds. I peek through a slit in the curtain to watch the audience fill the rows of seating and fill the space with expectant chatter and laughter to the overture medley of show tunes.

The auditorium lights dim, spotlights illuminate the stage, and the audience responds with hushed, mesmerized, silent attention. The curtain rises as Charlie the Christmas Fairy and Snowy the Snowman walk on from either side of the stage. They wait a few moments as the follow-spots shakily focus their beams of light.

"Good evening, ladies and gentlemen, boys and girls. And welcome to *The Christmas Spectacular*!" says Charlie, holding out her arms wide.

Snowy the Snowman nods along, smiles, then adds, "Who is feeling festive tonight?" He cups one of his hands to his ear in a dramatic pose of listening.

A few people shout back, but the snowman shakes his head, slumps his shoulders, and looks disappointed.

"What?" he yells back. "I can't hear you." Snowy steps forward. "I said, who is feeling festive tonight?" This time, he gets the response he's after and pretends to fall backward with the force of the noise. Everyone laughs. Snowy the Snowman is very funny.

I watch Snowy and Charlie sing their duet from the shadows, behind the plywood cutout snowman. James and I have been assigned scene-change duties, but I'm caught up in their song, 'Lonely This Christmas'. The sorrowful song reminds me that, after tonight, I won't be seeing James anymore. This is the end. I turn my attention briefly from the performers to my scene-shifting partner. James must have sensed my change of focus because he turns toward me. I can just make out the contours of his face. His eyes reflect the stage lighting. He smiles gently. Does he know that I'm feeling sad?

But there's no time to ponder. The cue for the scene change is coming up. I listen for the line, '*Some people don't believe in fairies*'. That's when James and I maneuver the plywood cutouts on castors and push them into place. I know the script, the line, and where it comes in the action, but I'm distracted by my feelings. When Snowy says the line, his words take me by surprise.

James nudges me. "Come on," he whispers, which snaps me into action.

I push one of the snow-covered hills into place, and James follows me with one of the beautifully painted and decorated snowmen. Locking on the brakes, I turn and see James's snowman almost topple over. It takes off on its own across the gently sloping stage and threatens to collide with the performers. Thankfully, James and I reach the runaway snowman in time. It tips on its edge, but we both wrestle to steady it and manage to keep it upright and stop it from toppling over. Out in front, I hear a collective 'Oooh-ahhh' from witnesses on stage. Behind the snowman, I help James secure the brakes, but something's faulty. They don't work.

We're out of time. The spotlight is on. The next song starts. The scene has begun. James and I cling to the runaway snowman. I don't think anyone in the audience is aware of our almost disaster, and, as long as we don't move, no one can see us. But now we're stuck on the stage, holding onto the snowman until the end of the second scene, when the snowman and the snowy hills get swapped for the interior cozy fireside with stockings and tree.

The action continues. James rearranges his arms around me as we hold on to the troublesome piece of scenery. We're so close. There are a few more minutes of fairies dancing before the mice come on. I listen out for the next scene-change cue, but it's not for a while yet. My hands start cramping up.

"Are you okay if I let go for a bit?" I whisper, turning my head slightly upward. "I'm getting cramp in my fingers."

"Sure. No problem. I've got it," James says close to my ear. The warmth of his breath sends tingles down the back of my neck. "The cue is coming up any minute."

James's strong arms are warm around my shoulders. Part of me wouldn't mind if we stayed right here for the rest of the show. The thought makes me smile.

But Charlie and Snowy launch into 'Baby, It's Cold Out-side', which prompts us to get moving. James and I wheel the faulty snowman off, stage left, and take a breather in the relative darkness. Scene three has begun. Cats and mice chase each other around in a chorus-line-type, high-kicking cancan, while singing 'Santa Claus is Coming to Town'. We have a few minutes before the next scene change.

"That was intense," I whisper. James leans toward me. He is so close in the dark, I sense rather than see him.

"Yeah. It's a good thing we got to it when we did," James whispers. "How are your fingers?"

"Thanks. I can feel them now," I say quietly close to James's ear. He turns toward me; his lips almost touch mine. I wonder if James knows how much I'd like to kiss him right now.

The cancan music stops. The stage lights change. Suddenly, Alfie appears close by, dressed in his elf costume; his face painted with a red circle on each cheek. I smile and give him a double thumbs-up. He comes over, hugs James, then one of the stage managers ushers him to wait behind a giant revolving Christmas cracker, ready to make his magical entrance onto the stage.

I shoot a glance at James, who is clearly feeling emotional about his son's performance.

"Are you okay?" I ask gently.

James doesn't answer but pulls me close and wraps me in a tight hug. I put my arms around him, leaning my head against his chest. He holds me and doesn't let go until a herd of children dressed as mice and cats darts past, our cue to shift the cozy interior to Rapunzel's tower, minus the faulty snowman.

# Chapter Four

## JAMES

"**A**lfie, you were fantastic!" I yell as my son, still dressed as Santa's elf, comes running into my arms. I scoop him up and swing him around. I'm so enormously proud.

Lester was right. The scene when Santa flies in on his sleigh was a showstopper. I peeked out at the amazed faces in the audience of open mouths and wide, shining eyes, and a collective gasp of wonder. Even though I knew about the mechanics of the crane, the effect was pure magic. The sleigh landed, Alfie and Santa got out and sang their number, 'Santa Claus is Coming to Town', then the elves and fairies joined in, tossing shiny wrapped gifts to each other like basketballs.

Watching from the wings with Flo, I was captivated. It was wonderful. She knew that I was overwhelmed by the whole thing. I don't know what I was feeling. A million emotions welled up inside me. Pride of seeing my kid on stage. Suddenly feeling alone. And sad because, after tonight, Flo and I would go back to how we were before.

Flo was right there beside me, so I reached out and hugged her. Of all the people in the world, at that moment, I knew she understood. She hugged me right back and we both stood there at the side of the stage, watching the show, wrapped in each other's arms, while Santa and his helpers sang and danced on.

Was this the Christmas spirit that I had heard about but never felt? The tingly, sparkly, giddiness that almost reduced me to tears?

Normally, I'm not an emotional person. But in that moment, a flood of feelings I had no control over gushed like a tsunami. I was grateful to be hidden in the darkness behind curtains and scenery. I was grateful that Flo was standing beside me, and when I hugged her, she hugged me back and didn't pull away. She fitted perfectly. Naturally. My chin resting on the top of her head. I felt safe. I felt happy. Filled with Christmas bliss.

When the song ended, we stopped hugging to clap and cheer. Flo was laughing and leaned toward me to say, "Alfie was brilliant!"

I couldn't speak. I was so proud, I didn't have words to express what I felt. Alfie and Santa walked to the front of the stage for a final bow and a standing ovation. Then, the curtain fell for the last time. The show finished. That was that.

Relief. Pride. Exhaustion. All the highs and lows of community Christmas theater wash over me. The audience is leaving, noisily singing along to the outro tune, 'Frosty the Snowman', and everyone on the stage – performers, technicians, stagehands, wardrobe, and props people jump up and down in a massive group hug, yahooing, shouting, and laughing.

Alfie runs toward me, shouting, "Dad! Did you see?"

I scoop him up in my arms and swing him around amongst the after-show celebration and mayhem. Looking around for Flo, I see her hugging Briana on the other side of the stage. She looks up and catches me, so I smile and wave. Alfie, still in my arms, waves to her gleefully with both hands. Lester climbs up a ladder and calls everyone to attention. I put Alfie on his feet but hold him close.

"Darlings," Lester says, smiling broadly. "We. Did. It." He punches the air.

The volunteers around me cheer and yell, "Yeah!" The atmosphere is jubilant and triumphant.

"Well done, everyone! You should all be very proud of yourselves." He smiles and tracks his eyes across the sea of upturned faces. "So, tonight is all about celebration, but only after the clean-up."

At the mention of clean up, the excited energy sags.

"Parents are exempt, of course," Lester says. "Get your child-stars home immediately. It's way past bedtime." He blows a kiss.

I look down at Alfie, who yawns and rubs his eyes. "Come on, buddy. Let's go, huh?" I tousle Alfie's hair. He nods wearily and holds my hand as we head to the green-lit exit above the stage door. We're almost there when Tony stops me.

"Hey, I just wanted to say thanks for all your hard work and dedication." Tony forcefully shakes my hand. "And you, Alfie, were fantastic."

Tony is closely followed by Briana and their two girls, who are still dressed as gingerbread people. They squeal and chatter as they go. Flo walks beside Briana.

"Alfie, you were amazing out there tonight," says Flo, grinning, clearly impressed.

"Thanks, Miss Simmons," Alfie says, looking up at his teacher.

"You really were," says Briana. "That sleigh scene was the best."

Alfie slides behind me, overwhelmed by all the adulation.

"We'd better get going," I say, as overwhelmed as my kid. "We've had a big day."

"Sure," says Flo, glancing from Alfie to me. I hold her gaze. Something in her expression is hard to read. Flo smiles but there's sadness behind her eyes. She looks away. I want to talk to her, to say how much I appreciate her kindness; to tell her how special she is; to say that I hope we can still be friends. I want to tell her about the letter from

Mrs. Claus and the way it has made me reconsider what I want for myself and for Alfie.

The cream-colored envelope is still in my pocket. It's comforting in its warm words of wisdom.

The first time I read it through, I was still certain that it was a prank from someone I knew because of the personal details it contained. Indignantly, I scrunched it up, threw it in the trash, and walked away. But then, I quickly regretted my action, pulled it out, smoothed the creases, and read it over again. The last sentence resonates and, as if someone has turned on a light, everything has become clear.

*Love is the greatest gift. Unwrap it with courage.*

I want to find the courage to explain to Flo what this means to me and see if she understands. But now is not the time.

"So," Briana says brightly. "Tony, take the girls home." She nods to her daughters to leave with her husband. "I'm going to help with the clean up and get a ride home with Flo, alright?"

"Oh, okay. Are you sure?" says Tony, reaching for the girls' hands. The sparkly effect of performing is wearing off like a fairy's magical spell. The children yawn and look sleepy.

"Yep," Briana says adamantly. "Oh, and we'll see you at our little get-together, James, won't we?"

"Me too," says Alfie, peeking out from behind my legs.

"Sorry, darl. Grownups only."

"I'll come if I can get a sitter for Alf. We'll see," I say to Briana, smiling despite the twist in my gut as Flo looks at the floor.

Maybe she knows what I feel for her. Maybe, like me, she is wondering what will happen next between us. Or perhaps she's a little embarrassed by my emotional openness when I hugged her. I hope Mrs. Appleby is still available to take care of Alfie at the weekend, so I can go to the after-party. I'd like to talk to Flo without my son's prying eyes.

A knot of children with their parents noisily pushes past and clatters through the exit door. I take Alfie's hand, and we turn to follow them out into the chilly night's air.

# *Chapter Five*

# FLO

"So, congratulations to all the stars who were in *The Christmas Spectacular*," I say, smiling around at the excited faces of my class after registration. The children are sitting on the mat in front of me, trying to be good, but fidgety with unsaid comments. It's best to move along quickly to the day's planned activities - creative, hands-on art project with a Christmas theme, of course - before the potential time-bomb of child energy explodes. Any school curricula learning is out of the window. After the theater performance last weekend, I know I have about a minute before the room becomes abuzz with little voices talking about the show. But before I can refocus on instructions for the activity, eager hands shoot up. I take a deep breath.

"Yes, Gabby. Do you have something important to say?" Gabby is a bright girl with good vocabulary. She's a safe bet.

Gabby folds her arms across her chest. "I liked it when the curtain opened at the start, and Alfie was the best elf," Gabby says boldly, nodding to Alfie, whose cheeks glow bright beetroot.

"Yes. Yes, Alfie was the best!" someone yells loudly, out of turn.

I hold out my hands, palms down, suspended in the air, as if the action is somehow going to put a lid on the unruly behavior. "Alright. But we don't call out, do we?" I shake my head. "No." Then I say, "Without saying anything, raise your hand if you agree with Gabby." A sea of hands shoots to the ceiling. "Fantastic. I agree too. But we have a busy morning, so I need you to pay attention and listen carefully." I wait for calm to resume.

The show is a great topic for an art project, and to explore vocabulary around theater and performing, as well as Christmas, of course. It also complements the letter-writing unit we completed, where each child wrote a letter to Santa.

The children in my class love anything creative and usually dive in, furiously drawing and coloring with pencils, pens, pastels, and crayons.

While I still have everyone's attention, I explain what is going to happen. "When you go back to your seats, you'll have thirty minutes to draw your idea about the show." I check the clock on the wall above the door and point out where the hands will be in thirty minutes. "You could choose your favorite moment. Or the character you liked the best."

"I'm going to draw Alfie," says someone, followed by some giggling, which I ignore.

I press on. I look from one child to the next, noticing how quickly the morning is slipping away. We've done this sort of activity many times, so the children should know what to expect. I begin with a visualization to help the children with recall and to clarify details of the show.

"Alright, then. Before we move back to our tables, let's think about the show and what it was like." I stand and slowly walk around the class. "What colors do you remember? What characters were on the stage? What happened to make you smile? What songs did you like?" I keep my voice soft and regular. "Children on table six, please quietly go to your chairs." The four children from table six stand up and instantly start chatting. "Oh, no. Children from table six, please sit down again." I shake my head and look disappointed. "Too much noise." The children from table six shoot each other daggers of accusation.

This always happens. Children need constant reminders about behavior and our 'no talking' rule. I place my hands on my hips and gaze around at the children. "Who thinks they can walk to their table without making a sound?"

Some children sit up straight with arms crossed, desperate to get my attention. Their lips are reduced to a thin horizontal line, as if the effort of keeping their voice in is making them force their mouths tight shut.

"Let's try table three. Children from table three," I whisper, "...please make your way to your chairs without making a sound."

This time, four children move across the classroom and arrive at their table without uttering a syllable.

"Excellent. Well done. Did you see how easy that was?"

Table by table, my class reposition themselves on their chairs and begin scribbling wildly, colors and shapes. They are supposed to wait for me to say start, but they are all on task, so I let it go.

I give the children a few minutes to settle into the activity, then I wander the room, offering encouragement and praise to keep the creative momentum. For some children, the drawing part of the project is all finished in less than five minutes. Asking questions prompts exploration of their idea. Some children need time to think about what they want to convey with their picture. I suggest adding details, speech bubbles, labels, and captions.

When I call time up, some of the children object. But then, eventually, everyone puts down their pens and pencils and sits at their tables, quietly, with arms folded. I choose some sensible helpers to collect each sheet of paper and, using magnets, fix them to the display boards around the room. Each artist will be invited to talk about their picture and answer questions.

"Wow! This is the best set of pictures I've ever seen," I say, walking around the pop-up art gallery. "We have so many ideas, everyone. These are really beautiful. I can see so much care and attention." I give my class a few moments to take in the exhibition, then I invite one of the children to nominate the first artist to share.

"I choose Desmond," says Eloise, from table two.

"Desmond. Are you ready to talk about your picture?" I ask gently. "You can go first or nominate someone else to go before you."

Desmond is a shy boy. He doesn't say anything, but points at Eloise, which is the expected outcome.

"Eloise. Please stand beside your picture and tell us about it in two or three sentences." Eloise walks to the display wall. "Everyone else. What are you going to do?"

Hands shoot up to answer. "Alfie. Tell us what we're going to do while Eloise is talking."

"Listen, Miss."

"Yes. Thank you. It's important to listen. But if you have a comment or question, Eloise will choose two people, who are sitting nicely, when she has finished talking about her picture."

All I have to do is facilitate this part of the lesson and keep the discussion on track. However, things could easily disintegrate into mayhem because the children sometimes get carried away with inquiry. I have strict controls over who is speaking. Before Eloise begins her explanation, I remind my class about keeping comments positive. The children don't intend to be mean, but their questions and comments can sometimes be brutal if unchecked by me. I don't want to suppress freedom of speech, but I'm mindful of keeping my breaktime free from sorting out hurt feelings and tearstained drama.

Eloise patiently stands beside her picture and articulately tells the class about her beautifully drawn fairy with decorated wings. She's even added a speech bubble with, 'Do you believe in fairies?' and another speech bubble from the audience with, 'YES. YES. YES.' I'm ready with a whiteboard pen to write a list of vocabulary that the children may not know.

"Thanks, Eloise." I turn to the rest of my class and say, "If you have a comment or question for Eloise, please raise your hand and she may choose you to answer."

As expected, Donna, Eloise's best friend, puts up her hand. No one else does, so Eloise says, "I choose Donna." There are a few groans from other children who predicted this outcome.

Donna says, "I love your picture. And I liked that bit the best, too." Donna has also drawn a fairy with speech bubbles.

"Thank you, Donna." I nod and smile. "Everyone is listening very well this morning. I like this calm classroom. You are making me a very happy teacher. Let's see if we can keep this going until recess." My hopes are slim, but it's good practice to comment on favorable behavior. I turn to Desmond, who avoids eye contact. "Desmond. Are you ready to tell us about your picture?" Desmond shakes his head. "Okay. Who would you like to go next?" Desmond points to Alfie.

"Alfie. Please stand beside your picture and tell us about it."

Alfie beams at me and scurries to stand beside his manically colorful piece of paper. It is colored so energetically, the paper is creased and ripped a little at the edges. Unlike Eloise's fairy, it's not evident what is happening in Alfie's picture, but I smile and nod for Alfie to begin.

"This is the stage." Alfie points. "Here's my dad." Alfie directs our attention to a stick figure at the side in a dark area. "And this is you, Miss Simmons," says Alfie, beaming at me. I peer at the scribble and can just make out another stick figure, slightly smaller than the first. Looking closely, I see that the stick figures appear to be embracing.

A collective gasp propels around the room like an audible Mexican wave, and someone calls out, "Alfie, are they holding hands?" Someone else says loudly, "Is your dad kissing Miss Simmons?"

I'm perplexed by this inquisition and slow to react.

Donna turns to me and says, "Miss Simmons. Are you Alfie's dad's girlfriend now?"

For a moment, all I can do is stare at my student. Her earnest blue eyes plead for an answer. I quickly shake my head. "No, Donna. I'm not."

She appears disappointed by this news, turns to face Alfie, and shrugs, while I watch as the peace and calm of my classroom erupt into shouts, squarks, and giggles.

Desperately, I flick a glance at the clock. Voices rise in volume as the discussion about my relationship with James Hadley spirals out of control. No one is listening to my calls for quiet. I bravely hope that the principal isn't choosing this moment to show new parents around the school. If anyone were to peep through the window, they would see a class in uproar and a teacher with absolutely no influence whatsoever.

"Enough," I yell above the din, but still, no one listens. I turn on the laptop and hurriedly find the link to 'Silent Night', a Christmas song we all know. I begin singing and encourage the children to sing along with me. When I have a critical mass of singers, I turn down the volume, and eventually I mime fingers on lips, which finally returns tranquility to the classroom.

"Oooh. That was too much noise. What just happened?" I use my sternest teacher voice for the rhetorical question. I don't want to go into explanations or excuses. Then, redirecting focus away from Alfie's picture, I point at the clock and say in a softer tone, "Now, I can see that it's almost time for recess." Thankfully, the bell for morning recess sounds. "Alfie, can you stay behind? Everyone else, quietly line up at the door. No talking. Keep your hands by your sides."

# *Chapter Six*

## JAMES

I am looking forward to life returning to normal after *The Christmas Spectacular*. My brain is fried. I don't remember ever feeling so tired. My idea of heaven, right now, is a few days of doing absolutely nothing. Or as near to nothing as I'm allowed because, I have learned, there is no downtime to being a parent. And being Alfie's dad? It is full on, twenty-four-seven.

*The Christmas Spectacular* ate into my time and energy, no doubt about that. But volunteering on the show was so much more fun and more rewarding than I thought it would be. Seeing my kid in his starring role was priceless. And sharing time with Flo? An unexpected, wonderful added extra. The rehearsals, constructing sets and props in the workshop, would not have been as fun without her. I even found myself looking forward to putting on my coveralls and being a slave in a cold, drafty workshop, just because I knew that she would be there.

Now that the show is over, I'm not sure how we're going to connect. I'd love to see Flo socially, but outside of theater activity, we don't share common ground, apart from the parent–teacher dynamic which, let's face it, does not bode well for a relationship beyond accepted professional norms.

I turn the idea of a future with Flo over in my mind. She is perfect and lovely and so easy to be around. Sadly, whichever way I look at us, the stats just don't add up. However, memories of us wrangling the runaway snowman and our almost kiss in the shadows are vivid and present all the time. Her warm arms around me when we hugged were real and left me wanting more.

I should let it all go. Move on. Wake up to reality, where the only interaction possible with Flo Simmons is at the next school function. Any kind of romance is off the cards and doesn't seem likely at all. But try telling that to Alfie.

My son likes his teacher probably as much as I like her, and he's been at me continually since I casually mentioned that I thought Miss Simmons was a 'nice person'.

This morning, when I was trying to get him out to school, he dropped another little nag into the conversation about how great it would be to see Flo at breakfast after a sleepover. I wince and cough as a mouthful of hot coffee hits my nostrils.

Recovering a little, I manage to swallow and say, "Alfie. Things are different for grownups." I put my coffee mug on the kitchen counter. "When you're a kid, it's okay to have friends for a sleepover. But..." I exhale and think about what I'm trying to say. "It's not what you do when you're an adult."

Alfie doesn't look convinced, and I can see him forming an argument.

"Hey, I bet you're excited about soccer this weekend?" It's a diversion tactic. Usually, the mention of soccer is enough to steer a conversation, but today it lacks its potent magic. I feel like Aladdin, desperately rubbing the lamp, hoping for a genie to appear. I sip my coffee and think of another distraction, but Alfie is like a terrier with a stick and brings the subject back with musings of what kind of breakfast Flo might like.

"Dad, do you think she eats Cheerios or toast?" Alfie says, studying the cereal packet before shaking out some of the contents. "Perhaps we could find out and have her favorite cereal in the pantry, just in case."

"Hey. Enough chat," I say, keeping my voice steady. "Eat up, or we'll be late again."

Hurriedly, I put the dishes in the dishwasher, wipe down the table, then I scoot around to the grocery list that's stuck on the fridge between a selection of Alfie's artworks, invoices, outstanding accounts, utility bills, and photos.

"We need to get some supplies after school, okay?" I read my list aloud as I scribble with a blunt pencil, *kitchen towels, cheese (a selection of), dips & chips, Christmas crackers, chocolate coins, laundry detergent, ham, potatoes.* If I didn't write down things that we needed, then I'd come home with everything that we didn't. "Can you think of anything else?"

"Ummmm." Alfie taps the side of his head with a forefinger. "Nope. I think you got it all, Dad. But can we get some Cheerios? I think Miss Simmons would like Cheerios." I rip the list from the notepad, fold it, and put it in my jacket pocket.

"Are you finished?" I say, reaching for Alfie's empty cereal bowl to put into the dishwasher.

Alfie hops down from the stool. "Yup." He takes a breath and looks as if he's about to say something else, but I cut him off.

"School bag. Shoes. Tied up properly, remember?" I check my watch. "Brush your teeth. Leaving in exactly three minutes. Go."

\*\*\*

That was this morning, and I foolishly believe that by the time I pick Alfie up after school, I've heard the last of his 'Let's invite Flo over' notions. But Alfie has other ideas. I drive to the grocery store, slow down to pull into a parking bay, and cut the engine. The shopping list is in my pocket.

Opening the car door to let Alfie out, he says hopefully, "Do we need more chocolate Santas for the tree?"

"No. I think we have plenty." I take my son's hand, and we walk together to the entrance, where I grab a cart and think of other items I may have forgotten.

Inside, my concentration is hampered by jolly Christmas music and busy shoppers stocking up on Christmassy items. Every aisle is floor-to-ceiling crammed with gaudy *Season's Greetings* packaging, stars, cheery Santas, elves, and reindeer.

"Do you think Flo has chocolate Santas on her tree?" asks Alfie as I push the cart along, mesmerized by the sensory overload of noise and shiny red wrapping, crowding in on all sides.

"Yes. Probably. I think it's pretty usual," I say, trying to focus on grocery shopping and not think about Alfie's cute teacher.

"I wonder what else she has. Do you think she has an angel or a star at the top of her tree?"

"I really don't know, Alfie. Maybe you could ask her at school." In the beverage aisle, I stop to grab a couple of bags of coffee beans and packets of tea. I'm about to move along when a parent of one of the players on Alfie's soccer team comes over.

"Hey! We saw you in the show last weekend, Alfie," he says. "You were great! Probably the best Santa's elf I ever saw in a Christmas show."

"I think you're right," I say proudly as Alfie grins up at me. I tousle his hair. "He was the best."

The jolly dad smiles, then says that he's got to get going. "Merry Christmas!" He waves and continues on his way.

"See. You're famous now," I say, pushing the cart around the end of the aisle. "Better get used to it."

"It's still a bit weird," says Alfie. "Funny that we don't have rehearsals anymore. What are we going to do with all our free evenings now we don't have a show?"

"I have some ideas, bud," I say, thinking about catching up on the games I've missed.

I peruse the shelves, looking for labels I recognize. Alfie, of course, picks up things we absolutely don't need and are not on my list.

"What about this, Dad?" he says, holding a Christmas bumper-pack of Oreos.

"Nope." I keep walking. Alfie trails behind.

"Dad."

"Yep."

"You know Ethan's dad just now. He seems pretty happy, huh?"

"Uh-huh." I reach for a double pack of kitchen towels.

"Ethan told me that his dad has started dating and things are going very well." I'm half-listening and trying to think of other domestic essentials that I've forgotten to write on the list that's still in my pocket. "He says that his dad isn't grumpy anymore and he has bought Ethan and his brother loads of cool game subscriptions."

"That's great."

"Ethan says his dad takes them bowling with his new girlfriend and then they go to Taco Bell, which is cool."

"Yes. That is cool." I load the cart with jars of peanut butter, strawberry jelly, sliced bread, tortilla wraps, and granola bars. Then I push the cart around to the next aisle and add flour, sugar, butter, and chocolate chips because I've been tasked with supplying chocolate chip cookies for Briana and Tony's after-show party.

"Hey, Dad. There's Flo," says Alfie, tugging my sleeve. "I'll go and say hi." My heart jolts like it always does at the mention of Flo, but I squish it down as Alfie scampers off behind the shelves, before I can form an excuse for him not to. In the blink of an eye, Alfie reappears, guiding Miss Simmons my way through a crowd of Christmas shoppers.

I'm feeling a little self-conscious because the last time I saw Flo, I was experiencing some sort of emotional breakdown. I pretend to be preoccupied with an item on the top shelf, which I realize too late is a giant pack of diapers.

"Alfie's a little old for those, don't you think?" Flo says, smirking and looking down at my son, who covers his mouth to stifle a snigger.

"Hey, Flo," I say casually, putting the pack of diapers back on the shelf, as if I do this all the time. "How are you? Fully recovered from *The Christmas Spectacular*?"

"Almost," she says, smiling. "It's strange to think that we don't have rehearsals anymore." There's a pause as Flo glances from me to Alfie. I sense a change in her expression from light-hearted to something resembling concern. "James. Can we talk?" She tilts her head slightly toward Alfie, who is suitably distracted by a carton of chocolate milk and doesn't notice.

"Oh, sure." I nod, fully understanding that what she has to say is about my son. I'm hoping for the best but expecting the worst. I bend down and say quietly, "Hey. I forgot toothpaste. Do you think you could scoot around and find some?"

"Sure, Dad," Alfie says, grinning up at me. "I'll be right back," he winks at Flo, "... while you two catch up." Then he slowly walks backward, away down the aisle, disappearing behind a woman pushing a loaded cart.

"That kid," I say, laughing. "So, what's up? Has he been ripping out pages of his notebooks again?"

"James." Flo begins. Then she sighs, laughs, and tells me about the art project in class that morning. I listen wide-eyed, as if we are teenagers caught smooching.

"Oh, no. I'm so sorry." I shake my head. "I'll talk to Alfie and get him to apologize."

Flo smiles and says, "I spoke to him after class, and I think he understands that, well - you and I - we're friends, aren't we? I'm his teacher and you're his dad, so..." Flo coughs slightly. "I also said that sometimes grownups can be more than friends." She points to me and then back to her a couple of times. "But not in our case."

"Yes. Of course. I mean no." I comb my fingers through my hair, an unconscious action when I'm confused, embarrassed, or unsure. "Thank you for clarifying. Our grown-up world can be confusing for a child."

"Our grown-up world can be confusing for an adult," Flo says, laughing.

"True. Very true." A moment passes between us. Something soulful, regretful, and a little sad. I swallow hard. "He has a wild imagination, doesn't he?"

Flo nods. "Oh, yes. Wild."

"Listen. Thanks for being so understanding." I take a breath, then I say, "He really likes you."

"Well, I really like him. He's a great kid. Lively. And sometimes without boundaries. But he has a good heart. And you're a great dad."

"Thanks." I look at my shoes. "Sometimes I feel like I'm only just hanging in there." Flo touches my arm. I feel the warmth of her fingers through the fabric of my jacket. She steadies me. I feel suddenly calm. As if Flo's touch has special calming powers, all tension is gone. I breathe and relax.

Alfie comes back. He has a pack of toothpaste in each hand. "I got two. One each for you and me." He tosses them into the cart. "With all that chocolate and candy we're going to be eating, I think we need to brush more."

"Hey," says Flo. "An excellent idea. I'm going to get extra toothpaste too." Flo turns to leave, but then she stops and says to me. "I'll see you at Briana and Tony's party?"

"Yeah. Looking forward to it."

"Me too," Flo says. Then she laughs and looks at the groceries in my cart. "I'm pleased to see that you're taking your cookie duties seriously, James."

"Yup. I'm planning to make the best chocolate chip cookies ever, but we'll see how they turn out. I'm mildly optimistic."

"You can come over and give Dad a hand, if you want, Miss Simmons. And, by the way, what kind of breakfast do you like?"

"Haha. Miss Simmons has already said that she has a ton of stuff to do, so..." I pull Alfie toward me in the hope that he'll stop talking.

"Thanks, Alfie, but I'll pass this time." Flo is talking to Alfie, but her eyes drift up to meet mine.

I'd love for Flo to come over and bake cookies with us, but after the art project incident, I think it's best if we keep our distance. Alfie's already invested in our joint future. I don't want to embarrass Flo anymore with Alfie's well-meant but inappropriate imaginings.

Flo turns to walk away, leaving me feeling empty, the exact opposite of our shopping cart, which is full and almost overflowing.

# Chapter Seven

## FLO

After the day I've had, the last people I want to see at the grocery store are James and Alfie. But Alfie sees me before I see him. I don't have time to form an escape plan. Before I can turn and run to the exit, he's tugging my sleeve and leading me around to where his dad is reaching for a bumper pack of diapers.

Seeing James melts my heart. He is the most adorable man. The look of bemused embarrassment on his face is enough to stop me in my tracks. So, instead of running, I reflect on the classroom drama and decide that a grocery store aisle is probably a suitable neutral space for a nonjudgmental, informal parent-teacher chat. James sends Alfie on a toothpaste-finding mission, which frees me up to talk about the art project incident.

James listens intently. He seemed mortified that Alfie hadn't thought that maybe his picture wasn't appropriate to share in class. But we both know what Alfie is like. We shouldn't be surprised.

When Alfie comes back with the toothpaste, I'm about to leave when Alfie says, "Dad got a letter from Mrs. Claus."

"Oh really?" I tilt my head to listen to what might be next while looking at James. His brow knits together. He shrugs slightly. His hand rests on the outside of his jacket.

"Yes. In fact, you can read it, if you like," Alfie says, before turning his hopeful smile to James. "Can't she, Dad. It's right there in your pocket."

James seems alarmed and says, "Ha! It's just the shopping list, Alfie."

"Yes. But the letter is in there, too." Alfie darts to James's jacket and pulls out a folded cream envelope. "Look, Miss Simmons. It's from the North Pole." He points to the postmark. "And smell it." Alfie holds the letter up to my nose. I bend slightly to sniff the paper. "Ummm. Gingerbread," he says.

James is flustered. "Oh, that. Ha! It's a joke from someone. I thought it was Mrs. Appleby, but she's adamantly denying it."

"What does the letter say?" I ask, bypassing professional teacher filters.

"I'm sure Flo has a million things to do, Alfie," says James nervously. "Let's not keep her here longer than is necessary."

"No. You're right," I say, sensing that the contents may be private and not for sharing in a supermarket aisle.

But Alfie begins to read. "Dear James, I hope this letter finds you well and full of the spirit of Christmas." Alfie beams up at me, then holds out the letter. "Go ahead, Miss Simmons, why don't you read it?"

James nods, giving me permission to continue. Carefully, I take the crumpled piece of handwritten paper from Alfie.

Dear James,

I hope this letter finds you well and full of the spirit of Christmas.

A talented little elf wrote to me. He says that your heart is full of love, but you've been keeping it locked away.

All that locked away love is making you sad.

You've been hiding behind excuses and convincing yourself, and the little elf, that everything is okay. But everything is not okay.

Free your feelings. Give yourself permission to be happy. Listen for the jingle of your heart—it's calling you to love.

Christmas is a time for giving. And what better way is there to give than to open your heart to a special someone who makes you feel alive and loved in return?

You are a great dad but don't use that as an excuse not to love again.

Love is the greatest gift. Unwrap it with courage.

With mistletoe kisses and a heart full of hope,

*Mrs. Claus*

OPERATION
MISTLETOE
MATCH

P.S. I hear The Christmas Spectacular really is spectacular!

Dear James,

I hope this letter finds you well and full of the spirit of Christmas.

A talented little elf wrote to me. He says that your heart is full of love, but you've been keeping it locked away.

All that locked away love is making you sad.

You've been hiding behind excuses and convincing yourself, and the little elf, that everything is okay. But everything is not okay.

Free your feelings. Give yourself permission to be happy. Listen for the jingle of your heart—it's calling you to love.

Christmas is a time for giving. And what better way is there to give than to open your heart to a special someone who makes you feel alive and loved in return?

You are a great dad but don't use that as an excuse not to love again.

Love is the greatest gift. Unwrap it with courage.

With mistletoe kisses and a heart full of hope,

Mrs. Claus

P.S. I hear The Christmas Spectacular really is spectacular!

"That's a lovely letter, Alfie," I say, handing the letter back, feeling as if James has allowed me to see into his soul. His eyes search mine, trusting me with these heartbreaking sentences, so intimate and personal amid Christmas shoppers at a grocery store.

"Yes. But I don't really understand that bit about the gift. Do you, Dad?" Alfie holds out the piece of cream-colored paper.

"I think what Mrs. Claus is saying," James says, glancing at me, "… is to be grateful for having such a talented child." He retrieves the letter from Alfie's hand, folding it tenderly.

"That's probably it," says Alfie, closing his eyes and smiling. "It's cool she wrote that line about the show."

Something in Alfie's comment sets off alarm bells, and, judging by the look on James's face, he was hearing them too.

"So, Alfie. I have a question," I say, intrigued by the handwritten letter.

"Oh, so do I," says James in a harsher tone.

"This letter from Mrs. Claus…" I rephrase my thought. "How did Mrs. Claus know about the show?"

"Well, that's easy," says Alfie with an expression of condescension. "From the letter I sent her, of course."

"Yeah?" says James. "And when did you send a letter to Mrs. Claus?"

"Oh, a few weeks back. In class."

James looks at me as if I had engineered the joke letter. So, I ask Alfie to clarify 'in class'.

Alfie grins impishly, then he begins pacing and rubbing his chin as if he's a lawyer in court, summing up a case.

"A few weeks back, if you remember, Miss Simmons, you asked us to write a letter to Santa."

"Sure. I remember."

"You said that when we finished, we should post our letters in the classroom Christmas mailbox."

"That's right. Go on."

"You said that you would post all the letters to Santa at the North Pole."

"Yes. And I did." I turn to James to clarify. "There's an official address for letters to Santa. I do it every year. It's a fun letter-writing project. The children love it."

"So, Alfie," says James. "You wrote a letter to Santa and put it in the Christmas mailbox."

"Yes. I did. And I also wrote a letter to Mrs. Claus and put that in the Christmas mailbox, too. I asked Miss Simmons if Mrs. Claus lives at the same address as Santa, and she said, yes, she does. So, tadaah! Mrs. Claus wrote back." Alfie points to the letter as if addressing imbeciles. "*Operation Mistletoe Match.*" James and I both look from Alfie to each other and back to Alfie, who is obviously enjoying being center of attention. He folds his arms, grins as if he has solved the world's energy crisis, then says, "Isn't that great? She sent this letter to my dad, telling him to... oh, what's that bit again?" Alfie takes the letter from James, unfolds it, and scans to the bottom of the page. "*Love is the greatest gift. Unwrap it with courage.* Well, I think that bit means he should get a girlfriend."

The following day at school, after the children have left, I'm summoned to the principal's office. My heart sinks. I'm convinced that one of the children in class has been so traumatized by the art project incident, they have cried themselves to sleep, and concerned parents have called to complain about my teaching abilities and classroom management, or lack thereof.

"Come in and take a seat, Miss Simmons," says the school principal, Mrs. Juana Ramirez. She interlaces her fingers and leans forward onto her elbows, which are firmly planted on the desk in front of her. She breathes deeply. "I have an opportunity for you," she begins. I nod and wait for my boss to continue, bracing myself for the inevitable lecture. "I applied for funding at the start of the year, and I'm happy to say that it has been approved."

"Wonderful," I say, smiling and relieved. "Congratulations."

"Thank you. So, the purpose of this funding has two benefits. Number one, to strengthen our leadership team and, number two, to employ additional teaching staff." Ramirez nods slowly and spreads out her fingers wide. "Now is the time to reevaluate. I'll be finalizing the details over the next few days, but I'd like everything to move forward in the new term." I wonder what this has to do with me, but I don't interrupt. "Miss Simmons. Flo. I need someone I can rely on to run the day-to-day structure of the school and implement the community outreach initiative. It'll be challenging, but because this is a new role, you'll be designing the building blocks, if that makes sense. It's a middle-management role that demands accurate reporting, but equally, there is room for creativity and system implementation. I thought I'd ask you face-to-face because you are my first choice for the role. And of course, the pay scale will reflect the demands and responsibility. I'm yet to finalize figures but it'll be somewhere in line with a senior teacher's salary."

My eyes are wide with surprise. I was expecting a reprimand, not a promotion. "Mrs. Ramirez. This sounds exciting. Thanks for considering me, but..." Possibilities chirp and chatter around my skull. This promotion would be a step up, for sure. It's thrilling and daunting in equal measure.

"This is a brand-new role. Non-teaching, but you'll still be an integral member of staff." Mrs. Ramirez smiles broadly. "Listen. It's short notice, but I'd like a decision by the end of the week."

I head back to my classroom slightly dazed as Mrs. Ramirez's words echo in my thoughts. I shut the door. The empty classroom seems extra quiet without the students. Child-sized chairs are neatly tucked under tables. Only a couple of hours earlier, this vacant space was busy with noisy learning and classroom interactions. My eyes are drawn to colorful projects, posters, and artwork that are pinned to the walls and pegged onto wire strung across the ceiling. The idea of this not being my classroom anymore seems alien. Unreal. Not possible.

I walk to my desk in the quiet vacuum. The clock ticks. My head buzzes with possibilities. I pick up a pile of math books, open the first one, and settle into my chair. I try to focus on the task of marking and check that everyone has completed the homework. They haven't. I put the book down, lean back in my chair, and laugh skyward.

Someone knocks. It's Briana. She waves through the glass, then opens the door.

"Hey. Is this a bad time? You appear to be howling at the full moon."

"No. Come in. I was just laughing at the math answers, or lack of them." I hold up a virtually empty page. "The date's right. And the margin is beautifully straight."

"That's a good start."

"But no homework." I put the book down, shaking my head.

"You sound surprised." Briana laughs. "It's the end of term. Everyone is thinking about Christmas. Not math."

"You're right." I sigh. "I just feel as if I'm playing catch-up all the time."

"Yes. It's called teaching," Briana says quizzically. "Did you not know that 'playing catch-up' was part of the deal?" She laughs again, then perches on one of the tables close by. "So, I heard Ramirez was planning a little shake-up. We're getting a new teacher, and someone is up for promotion." Briana winks and looks sly. "Are congratulations in order?"

"Haha. Briana. I don't know." I hold my head in my hands. "There's so much to think about. She's just made me a verbal preliminary offer, but I don't know if I'm going to take it."

"What?" Briana jumps up. "Why?"

"The kids," I say, gazing around my classroom. "And I don't know if I'm ready."

"Ramirez wouldn't have asked you if she didn't think you were up to the task." Briana smiles. "Honestly. This is a fantastic opportunity. Grab it. It's yours." She walks to my desk and leans on both hands, looking me straight in the eye. "Let's face it. The kids aren't even going to miss you."

"Ah, thanks."

"You know what I mean. They're adaptable. And this new job is middle-management, so you'll be the go-to substitute teacher. No doubt about that." My friend smiles. "This is great, Flo. Do it." She tilts her head to one side. "You can always go back to classroom teaching, if you're really not happy."

"Thanks, Bri. You always make things clear."

"I am a very good teacher."

"True."

There's a beat, then Briana says, "The other major benefit of not being a classroom teacher is what, Miss Simmons?"

"Excuse me?"

"Don't tell me that you haven't considered what this promotion could mean for you and Mr. James *Dreamy* Hadley?" She looks at me with raised eyebrows, then slaps her thigh and says, "Flo. Come on! You two are great together. And, because you won't be Alfie's teacher anymore, it frees you up for proper dating without the off-limits label. Think about that, why don't you?"

I stare into space, trawling through all the other reasons why I shouldn't date James Hadley, but I can't come up with any. My head swims with vertigo. I feel as if I'm about to step off a very high cliff and there's nothing to stop me falling. Memories of the letter from Mrs. Claus flash like a strobe, releasing excited flutters of butterflies. I shake them away but '*upwrap it with courage*' repeats like a mantra.

Briana walks toward the door. She turns and says quietly, "What do you want for Christmas, Flo?" She pauses a second, then says, "It could be that James *Dreamy* Hadley wants the same thing too. It certainly appears that way from what I've seen. The only way you're going to find out, is if you ask him. Am I right? Or am I right?"

# *Chapter Eight*

## JAMES

Alfie and I are in the kitchen, preparing an area on the counter for baking, although I'm not sure what I'm doing. I have found a recipe for choc chip cookies that looks alright. Thankfully, Mrs. Appleby said that she would be happy to help and would stop by this evening. She really is a national treasure.

While Alfie and I are getting the kitchen cookie-baking ready, I reckon it's a good time to bring up the subject of the art project incident. I told Flo that I would talk to Alfie about it, and also, I'd like to hear about what happened from his side. I know my son wouldn't intentionally cause trouble, but he does have a wild imagination and often gets carried away.

"Could you please get the flour from the pantry?" I ask as I hunt for weighing scales. Alfie opens the pantry door and looks up and down. "Should be on the third shelf in a blue packet."

"This one?" says Alfie, holding a packet of corn chips in an orange packet.

"What a comedian." I lean against the kitchen counter, fold my arms, and pretend not to be amused. "You should be on the stage."

"I was," says Alfie, finding the flour and carefully placing it on the counter with both hands.

"Ah, yes. That's right. Remind me again?"

"No, Dad." Alfie laughs.

I pause for a minute, then I say, "Miss Simmons told me that something happened in art class." I hand Alfie a milk carton to put back in the fridge. He turns away from me, opens the fridge door, and places the milk inside. "Can you tell me what happened?"

Alfie closes the fridge door and climbs up onto the stool beside me. "I didn't think everyone would scream and laugh like they did."

"Oh, okay. What made them scream and laugh, do you think?"

"My picture."

"Alright. Can I see your picture?"

"No. It's in the trash."

"Oh, Alfie. That's no good. I like to see what you've been doing at school. Miss Simmons says you have a very good imagination. I think so too." I walk to the pantry and find the sugar and chocolate chips. Then turn back to Alfie. "Can you tell me about your picture? What did Miss Simmons ask you to draw?"

"She said to draw something about the Christmas show."

"Oh, great! There was a lot." I arrange the packets on the counter. "I remember the fireplace with the stockings hanging up, and the Christmas tree with all those presents wrapped up with shiny paper. And Santa flying in on a sleigh. Now. Help me out here. Who was with Santa in that sleigh? Someone famous, I think."

"Dad! It was me." Alfie laughs.

"Ah, yes. That would have been my picture. You in the sleigh with Santa." I hug my son, then ask gently, "So, what was your picture?"

Alfie takes a deep breath and lets it out slowly. "Promise you won't be mad."

"I promise."

"I drew the stage."

"Great! What else?"

"The big snowman."

"Fantastic. Is that it?"

"No."

"What else?"

Alfie examines the edge of the countertop and says, "I drew you and Miss Simmons."

"Okay. Why would I be mad about that?"

"Because..." Alfie runs his finger along the countertop edge, "... you and Miss Simmons were kissing."

I sit down on the stool next to Alfie. "Mmmm. I think this is what Miss Simmons means by very good imagination, Alf." I put my arm around my boy and hug him. "You know when something seems like it's real, but it's only..." My voice trails away.

"It looked like you wanted to kiss her, Dad." Alfie looks earnestly into my eyes.

I shake my head. How am I to explain the complexities of emotions to my kid? Yes. Alfie has a wild imagination, but he also sees right through my pretence. I did want to kiss Flo, but Alfie can't hear that from me. I collect my thoughts, so I sound reasonable. Sensible adult thoughts. A grown-up way of thinking.

"Remember the presents under the tree in the show?"

"Yup."

"They looked like real presents, didn't they? Shiny, colorful paper. Big fancy bows. Labels telling us who they were for. But it was just pretend. Just for the show. We know that there was nothing inside. Just empty cardboard boxes."

Alfie stares at me for a moment, his brow knits together in thought. Then he says, "But Flo is your friend. She's real, and I know you like her a lot, and she likes you." Alfie reaches into my pocket and forcefully pulls out the letter. "Here. Read this again!" Alfie says with more than usual volume. "Read what Mrs. Claus is telling you. I wrote that you're sad. I said that you spend all your time working and not having fun. But when you were helping on the show, you did have fun. And that was because Miss Simmons made it fun."

"Hey, Alfie." I attempt to regain the higher ground. "But we have fun, don't we? Just us. You and me." I'm saying the words to convince myself more than my son.

"Yup, Dad." Alfie gets down from the stool. "I guess," Alfie says with disappointment that cuts right through me.

He's right, of course. Before I got to know Flo, I believed that Alfie and I were all we needed to be happy. But since the show, I've had a massive change of heart. Alfie knows I'm bluffing.

"The thing is, Flo – Miss Simmons – is your teacher, and there are rules about getting to know your teacher too well."

"Like, she might give me the answers to the exam questions? Or give me better grades than the other kids?"

"Something like that. Yes."

Any further discussion regarding my non-existent love life and romantic possibilities with Alfie's off-limits teacher is put on hold because there's a knock at the door. It's Mrs. Appleby.

"Edna," I say, standing aside to let my neighbor in. "Thank you so much for helping out."

"Oh, my pleasure." Alfie runs and hugs Mrs. Appleby, then looks back at me as if I'm an ogre. "Alfie! Are you alright?" Mrs. Appleby says, reaching a kindly hand down to stroke his hair. Alfie doesn't say anything but buries his face in Mrs. Appleby's cardigan. "Now, James. I don't know which recipe you have. And I hope you don't think I'm interfering, but I brought my favorite tried and tested, no-fail, Christmas choc-chip cookie recipe." She pats her purse.

"Edna. Thank you so much." Mrs. Appleby releases herself from Alfie and follows me to the kitchen. "What can I get you? Tea? Coffee? Some sherry perhaps?"

"Ooh, James. Maybe later. When the cookies are baking," Mrs. Appleby says, smiling at me. Then she turns to Alfie. "I think this recipe needs some Christmas magic. Do you know any elves that could help us?"

"I know the best one," I say, smiling at my son and crossing my fingers that he has forgiven me. Thankfully, Alfie smiles back, although its usual joyous cheekiness is lacking. "Alfie, why don't you show Mrs. Appleby our tree?"

"You have a tree! How wonderful. Then Christmas really is coming," Mrs. Appleby says, beaming. She holds Alfie's hand as he leads her to the living room. "And tomorrow, we'll have a great time, while your dad is at the grown-ups-only party. I'll make sure we bake enough cookies tonight for you and me to decorate tomorrow. Alright?"

"Yeah, Mrs. Appleby. We'll have our own party, right here, and have way more fun than the grown-ups."

Edna glances back at me. I put my grateful hands together as if I'm praying and mouth a silent *Thank you*.

# Chapter Nine

## FLO

B riana dings her glass with a teaspoon and waits for the excited chatter to settle. "Honestly. You're worse than the kids in my class," she says, laughing. "Can I have your attention. Please!" Briana is wearing a silver tinsel crown and fairy wings and is standing precariously on a chair in the hall. "Now that everyone is here, or nearly everyone, Tony and I would like to welcome you all to our humble home," she says, smiling at her husband, and managing to curtsey, only wobbling slightly.

A party popper is popped, showering its colorful string over Briana's glittery hair. A couple of people cheer and whistle. She waves a hand to indicate she has more to say.

"Just a couple of things. Firstly, a huge congratulations to everyone involved with *The Christmas Spectacular*!" Raucous shouts, cheers, and whistles explode from her assembled guests. "A big thank you is in order to Lester, our eminent master and commander," Briana finds Lester in the crowd and raises her glass. Lester smiles, bows his head, placing a hand on his heart, "... for inspired direction and pulling the whole crazy thing together. I believe I speak for everyone – cast, crew, and slaves – when I say that this year's Christmas show has been The Best Ever!"

Another raucous cheer erupts, and guests enthusiastically applaud Briana's sentiment. She waits a few minutes for order to resume before she continues.

"So, thank you all for coming. I hope you have a great night and a safe and very merry Christmas!" Briana ends with both hands raised in the air to a rapturous ovation.

"Wonderful speech, Bri," I say, holding out my hand to help my friend down off the chair amid noisy chatter and loud laughter. Someone blows a party whistle, while someone else snaps another party popper, releasing more colorful streamers over our heads.

Briana puts her glass on the table and grabs me in a bear hug. "Thank you, gorgeous girl," she says, beaming. She kisses my cheek, then she dramatically searches left and right. "So, where is the wonderful Mr. Hadley?"

"I'm not sure if he's coming tonight."

"Not sure?" Braina says, gasping. "Of course, he's coming tonight. It's the wrap party. He's not going to miss this fun night and the chance to pull a cracker with you." Briana holds out her hand for me to shake. "Would you like to make a bet? Twenty bucks says that he'll be here."

I laugh. "He may not have found a childminder for Alfie. He's a parent, you know, with responsibilities."

"I'm a parent with responsibilities!" Briana picks up her glass and sips her champagne. "Although I am eternally grateful to obliging grandparents for taking care of the girls this weekend, so mommy can let her hair down. Cheers!" She sips again, then her free hand shoots up in mock horror. "Shame on me, Flo. You don't have a drink." Briana steers me toward the kitchen. "What can I get you? We have everything. Tony has done a brilliant job of setting up a fully stocked bar."

Briana and I zigzag through knots of cheerful guests to the refreshments table in the kitchen, where she pours me a glass of bubbly wine from one of the open bottles in an ice bucket.

"Here's to your new job," Briana says, smiling. I open my mouth to say something about nothing set in stone yet, but she goes on. "Here's to new things of all sorts." She raises her glass. "Even if James doesn't come tonight, we are going to have the best time ever because we are fabulous." Briana grins at the ceiling. She hugs me again. "Listen," she says. "It's Mariah." She takes the glass from my hand, puts it on the counter by the sink, then steers me through the crowd in the hallway and yells, over her shoulder, "Come on. Let's carve up the dancefloor."

In the living room, the rug is rolled up and slumps on furniture that's pushed to the sides, leaving space in the middle for dancing. Briana and I join a crowd of others in colored party lights, who wave their hands in the air under a disco ball, and howl along with the well-loved Christmas lyrics. The final chords for 'All I Want For Christmas Is You' mix seamlessly into the next track, which is a slow song I don't recognize.

A tinkling piano plays under a soulful woman's voice who sings about following her heart and wondering if this Christmas she'll be loved. I think it's Norah Jones, but I can't be sure. Briana is swept away by some energetic guests who are convinced that fruity cocktails are a good idea, but I stay to listen to the song and watch as couples pair up and hold each other as they dance close together. I wonder what it might be like to slow dance with James.

"Hey, Flo," a familiar voice says close behind me, making me turn around. "I like your earrings." It's James. My heart leaps and I instinctively touch one of the mini sparkly Christmas trees that dangle from my ears. "You look beautiful," he says with a shy smile. "I mean, you always look beautiful. Even in coveralls."

"Thanks," I say, looking down at my red sequined shoes, feeling a little bit awkward in my party clothes. I'm even wearing makeup. Then, diverting attention from my appearance, I say brightly, "You made it."

"Yeah. I didn't want to miss tonight." James sweeps a hand through his hair. He looks away and exhales as if he's collecting his thoughts. "Would you like to dance? With me?"

I don't say anything. Just nod. Then, James takes my hand and leads me to join the other couples in the sprinkling of pink glittery light under the revolving mirror ball. The slow song continues, lilting from chorus to verse. I lean into James's strong arms and rest my head on his shoulder. His breath is warm on my neck. It's bliss. His fingers curl around mine. Our bodies move in time. Then, the sweet song ends and, as if we've been under a slow-dance spell, we break apart. But James still holds my hands.

"We had bets on that you wouldn't come," I say, suddenly aware of how many people are watching us. Shyly, James and I leave the dancefloor as 'It's Beginning to Look a Lot Like Christmas' begins.

"Finally, you two," says Charlie, who looks like a fairy even when she's not dressed in a sparkly dress and wings. "Does this mean it's official?"

"I don't know what you're talking about," I say, avoiding Charlie's question as James, still holding my hand, leads me through the crowd.

"Oh, come on," says Charlie, dramatically rolling her eyes to the ceiling. "Someone, anyone, please find some mistletoe for Flo and James." She laughs. "Just kiss, already."

I blush as we move along to the kitchen, and make-shift bar, which is packed with people who laugh and talk loudly. Everyone's having a great time. Tony is circulating through the hubbub, handing out flutes of champagne from a tray.

"Ah, there you are," he says, beaming as we enter the crowded little room. "Glad you could make it." Tony hands us each a glass filled to the brim with fizzy wine.

"Thanks, Tony," says James above the din. "This is a great party."

James and I raise our glasses to salute our host, then take a sip. Tony smiles as he maneuvers artfully through the merry throng, holding the tray at head height, and handing out more glasses of fizz.

"How come you thought I wouldn't make it?" asks James, leaning in close to me to be heard.

"Oh, well. You're a responsible parent. And reliable child minders are hard to come by this close to Christmas."

James laughs. "You're right. I am a responsible parent, but sometimes even a responsible parent is allowed to go to a party and have fun." He sips from his glass. "But I wouldn't be here without the amazing Mrs. Appleby."

"Ah, yes, our very own national treasure. A toast, then," I say, raising my glass. "... to the amazing Mrs. Appleby."

"Mrs. Appleby," James chimes in before we sip our champagne. Refreshing bubbles tickle my nose pleasantly.

"And are those your Christmas cookies?" I say, noticing an abundant arrangement of beautifully decorated double-decker cookies stacked high on a plate, dominating the refreshments table.

"Yes," says James. "I'm a bit proud of myself, although, once again, I have Mrs. Appleby to thank. She came over yesterday with her no-fail Christmas choc-chip cookie recipe. Alfie and I both tested them to make sure they were up to standard, and I can confidently confirm that they are. Please, have one."

"Maybe later, when I've finished my bubbly wine."

"There might not be any left by then," James says proudly.

"In that case, you might need to bake a special batch, just for me." The bold, unfiltered thought tumbles out of my mouth unchecked. Color rises to my cheeks. The effects of bubbly wine, no doubt. I glance up at James to gauge his reaction.

James holds my gaze and says quietly, "I'd be happy to, Flo. Yes."

The noise of the crowd melts away. We're wrapped in a moment of magical stillness where only James and I exist. A moment of intimacy, not unlike when we were stuck behind the snowman in the show, and we almost kissed. But the moment evaporates as Briana swoops into the kitchen to refill her glass.

"Ooh, they look scrummy," she says, helping herself to one of the chocolate chip double-deckers. She takes a bite. "Mmmm. We might need to hide these from the guests and eat them all ourselves." She munches another bite, then turns to James. "Has she told you her big news yet?" Briana says, nodding my way.

"No." I laugh along with my friend. "Not yet."

"News? What news?" James asks in between sips of champagne.

"Nothing is absolutely definite yet. But I'm not going to be teaching anymore."

"Oh no. What happened?" James looks worried. "Is everything alright?"

I laugh at James's concerned reaction. "Did you think that I'd been fired or something?"

"No. No, not that." He laughs. "I don't know what I thought. But you're a great teacher. The kids love you." After a beat, James says, "Alfie's going to miss not having you as his teacher. This year, he has come such a long way, and it's all because of you, Miss Simmons."

"Ha! It's not all because of me." I'm blushing at James's kind compliment. "Alfie's a smart kid. He'd do well anyway. With me or another teacher."

"Not true. Uh-uh." James shakes his head. "Alfie is hard work sometimes, but he'll do anything for you."

"Well, that's nice of you to say so."

"So, tell me. What is it that you're going to be doing?" asks James. "Not leaving town, I hope."

"No. I'll still be at school, but I've been offered a promotion, a non-teaching role, and after a great deal of consideration and advice from my friend here," I nod to Briana, "... I've decided to take it."

"Isn't that wonderful?" says Bri, glass in one hand, cookie in the other.

"Congratulations, then," says James. "Here's to you, Flo Simmons. All the best in your new job."

"Thank you," I say happily, feeling a bit giddy. But it's not just the bubbly wine or the lively theater crowd or James *Dreamy* Hadley standing in front of me, being incredibly - but casually - handsome, and toasting my future. It's all of it. Everything. I feel like a glass, full of bubbly wine, spilling over with effervescent happiness.

"Enough of that," Briana says, putting her glass down on the table. "Listen." She cups a hand to her ear. "It's 'Rocking Around the Christmas Tree'. Come on. Let's go dance."

# *Chapter Ten*

## JAMES

It's not late. But I feel like I should leave soon so Mrs. Appleby can go home. I hope that she has survived an evening with Alfie and nothing major has happened. She hasn't called me, so that's a good sign.

The party is pumping. The dancefloor is packed. I watch Flo, who is chatting with Lester and others, although typically, he is holding court. Flo is so incredibly pretty tonight. I'm captivated by her. Mrs. Claus's words revolve through my mind and, unconsciously, my hand smooths the outside of my jacket pocket, making the letter crinkle inside. As if Flo senses me watching, she glances up, smiles, then comes over to me.

"I was wondering if I could walk you home." The words surprise me. They come out on their own. Loud. Uninvited, like something Alfie might say. I've enjoyed the party and celebrating with everyone, but I'd really like to be alone with Flo now. "I mean, when you're ready, we can walk together, from here to your house," I say, trying to make the idea seem sensible, but I'm gabbling.

"That would be nice. Thanks." Flo tilts her head, her eyes light up. "I was planning on walking. It'll be good to have company." She smiles. "No chance of getting a cab on the Saturday before Christmas, so no point in trying, huh?"

"That's true."

"Well, if you're ready to go now, I am," Flo says. "I'll just get my coat and say goodbye to Bri and Tony."

I follow Flo back to the hall, where I find my jacket under a pile on a chair. Flo finds hers in a bundle on the hatstand. Music still stomps from the living room where Briana waves, then, seeing we're about to leave, charges over pulling Tony by the arm.

"You're leaving too soon, party-poopers!" Tony says, wrapping his wife in an enormous hug.

"Maybe they're going to another party. Although I believe that this is the only one worth going to tonight." Briana reaches out to kiss Flo on her cheek. "Take care. I'm pleased you have a bodyguard with you; otherwise, I'd lend you mine." She bats her eyelashes at Tony cheekily.

"It's not far, Bri. I've walked home from your house a million times alone before. No big deal. But thanks for offering."

I shake Tony's hand, kiss Briana's cheek, and thank them for a great party. "Merry Christmas!"

"Merry Christmas, you two. We'll see you on the other side, no doubt," says Briana, then she turns to Flo and mimes, 'Call me'.

Our hosts wave as we exit, and I close the door behind us. Outside on the street, it's crispy cold and, compared to the party inside, so very quiet. My ears ring from the dancefloor music, and volume turned all the way up. My breath comes out in frosty clouds. I put on my knitted beanie and wrap my woolly scarf tight, twice around my neck.

Flo buttons her coat, shivers a little, and shoves her hands into her pockets. We begin to walk. Flo's house isn't far. We fall into rhythmic step, keeping a brisk pace as a way of warming up, rather than getting to the destination quickly.

"Your cookies were a big hit," says Flo, her voice slightly muffled in the upturned faux fur collar of her coat.

"They didn't look like the picture at all, but they turned out much better than I thought they would."

We walk along a few paces more. Flo tugs her collar up higher around her neck. "Wait a minute," I say, stopping to unwrap my scarf. I hold it out for her. "Here. Put this on. You're cold."

"No. I'm fine." Flo walks on a few paces.

"You're shivering," I say, moving to stand in front of her. "Let me."

Flo looks up at me with twinkling eyes. "Thank you, James," she says, as I carefully wrap my scarf around her shoulders, swamping her in warm wooliness. A strand of her hair has fallen loose. I stroke it back into place. It's silky smooth under my fingertips. Now it's me who is shivering, but it's not because I'm cold. We stand together, close under the lamplight. Our breath crystallizes then disappears in an instant.

"Flo," I begin. Then, I hesitate. I'm not sure what I want to say next. There are so many thoughts crowding my mind, each fighting to be out first. But I hush these pesky thoughts because the moment is perfect without words. I don't want to move on from where we are or alter anything about it.

Flo takes a small step toward me and, intuitively, I accept her into my space, reach down to take her hands, entwining her fingers in mine. She rests her head gently against my chest. It feels like the most natural thing in the world. As if she is meant to be there. Here, with me. I breathe in the scent of Flo's hair, the warmth of her skin, and relish our closeness out on the cold, shadowy, winter street. It's so very quiet and still. There's no one else around.

"You can keep the scarf," I say close to Flo's ear. "It's yours."

"Oh, thank you," she says, pulling the scarf a little tighter around her neck and shoulders. "An early Christmas present? How thoughtful."

"Yes. But I got you something else as well."

"You did?"

"Yes. But it's under our tree, so if you want it, you'll have to come to our place to get it. Alfie wrapped it up especially for you."

"Thanks. I'd love that. I have one for you, too."

"Really?"

"Yes. And for Alfie. I figured that, now I'm not his teacher anymore, it's alright to get him a gift without feeling guilty about not getting a gift for the other thirty kids in my class."

"That's right. You're not his teacher anymore. So..."

"So?"

"That means we can... I mean..." I squeeze Flo's hands, curling my fingers around hers. "Flo. Would you be okay with... Can I call you, and perhaps we can..."

"Yes, James. We can. And I'd love that." Happy tears have made Flo's pretty eyes swim. She grins and pulls me to her with both arms. "You have no idea how much I'd love that."

We hug for a moment, then Flo says, smiling up at me, "Hey, it's snowing."

A snowflake lands on Flo's hair. I carefully brush it away with my hand. Flo halts my action, pressing my fingers against her warm cheek. Then she turns her head to kiss my palm. A rush of warm tingles floods my senses. I cup Flo's pretty face in both hands. She closes her eyes as I bend to kiss her soft, rosy lips. Flo pulls back slightly, then, without hesitation, she kisses me back. We kiss, my lips on hers. This kiss that I have imagined for so long is real and magical. We meld with the swirls of snowflakes immersed in this beautiful moment of pure bliss, pure feeling. Flo leans into me as I wrap my arms around her, drawing her to me. The kiss goes on in muffled snow-filled silence.

When we eventually break apart, I whisper, "Do you want to know a secret?"

"Yep."

"I wanted to kiss you when we got stuck behind the snowman. Remember that?"

"I do!" says Flo. Her hands cover her mouth. "So, Alfie's picture was correct. Ten out of ten for observation, Alfie." She laughs and shakes her head, then links her arm through mine. "That kid. He's way too smart for his own good." We walk a few paces further on, then Flo says, "Hey, do you still have that letter. The one from Mrs. Claus?"

"It's right here in my pocket." I pull out the letter. It's creased and dog-eared from being handled: folded, and refolded. "Here." Flo takes the piece of cream-colored paper and holds it up to read.

"That last line," she says as we walk on a few paces more. "About the greatest gift being love and unwrapping it with courage. I've been thinking about that a lot, lately."

"She's right, you know," I say, putting my arm around Flo's shoulder and gently pulling her to me. "Love does take courage. It's a risk. A massive scary risk." I laugh. "You know, I've been making excuses about Alfie being too young and life being just fine as it is. And I've been trying to ignore that I am very attracted to his pretty teacher." I kiss the top of Flo's head. "But getting this letter - and because I know now that it's really from Alfie - I think I'm ready. I think I have the courage to take the risk." I stop and face Flo, holding her hands in mine. "With you."

Flo smiles. She reaches up and touches my lips with her fingertips. Then we kiss – deeply, passionately, without restraint as the wintry world revolves around us. Flo kisses me, and I don't feel like I am risking anything at all. I am hers. She has me totally. One hundred percent. I'm not scared. I'm not fearful, and I'm not being courageous. Falling in love with Flo feels like the most natural thing in the world; like something that is just meant to happen; like something written in the stars.

We start walking down the street again. The snow falls softly, absorbing any sound apart from our breathing and footsteps.

"It's a good thing that we didn't kiss behind the snowman on stage because the show would have been very different. One that Lester surely wouldn't recognize."

"I have to admit," says Flo, leaning into me. "I wanted to kiss you, too. That time behind the snowman and loads of other times."

"Oh yeah?" Our pace has slowed to a gentle amble. Despite the cold, we're in no hurry to arrive at Flo's house.

"Even that time when I saw you in the grocery store, when you had a multi-pack of diapers in your hands." Flo laughs and kisses me. "I thought then, that's the man for me. Absolutely irresistible."

Snow falls all around. It's getting heavier. The sidewalk has a white, crispy covering which crunches pleasantly beneath our feet.

# *Epilogue*

# FLO

## Not quite one year later...

The Woodhill Community Christmas Show was another triumph this year. James and I both volunteered, of course. Tony and Briana didn't because of their baby boy, Ewan, who arrived in November. He was a big and unplanned surprise for his parents. His older sisters adore him, and both mom and baby are doing well. And Tony? Briana says he's still in shock but getting used to the idea.

Alfie was in the show. He was a shepherd, a tropical fish, a shooting star, and a Christmas cracker. Chorus-line parts, but he excelled in them all.

"I hope it snows again this year," says Alfie when we haul the tree into James and Alfie's living room. It's the biggest one we could find, and it takes up most of the space. James, Alfie, and I spend a happy afternoon decorating the voluminous tree with festoons of fairy lights, garlands of tinsel, and glittery figurines on golden loops of string. Typically, the tree is overdone, like an explosion in a Christmas decoration department, but that's what to expect from Alfie. He doesn't do halfway.

"Pass me your star, Alfie," says James, climbing up the stepladder. "It's going to make ours the best Christmas tree this side of the North Pole."

Alfie passes his dad a giant sequined, multi-sided, cardboard star. James uses a length of bendy wire to attach it to the top of the tree.

Alfie and I both applaud the finishing touch as James climbs down the ladder. We clear away the decoration boxes and turn on the fairy lights. The tree is stunning.

I don't miss being a classroom teacher at all. My new role took some getting used to, and there was a lot to learn at the start. But Juana was always supportive, and the rest of the staff were there to help out, too, so moving into next year will be a breeze.

James and I have been dating. Although I'd say we're a bit further on than just dating. The only way I can explain it is that we just seem to fit. It's not an effort to be together. He is my best friend, the person I'd rather be with than anyone else in the whole world, and I know he feels the same about me. We are truly, madly, deeply, blissfully happy and looking forward to the next step, which I believe is packaged up in a little box, on one of the tree branches, in shiny paper, with a fancy bow and a label that reads, *'To Flo. Merry Christmas with all my love, James'*.

"You can open this now, if you want," says James, reaching for the small shiny cube.

"Yes, Flo. Open it!" yells Alfie, jumping up and down.

"Is that allowed? If I open my present now, then I won't have a present to open on Christmas morning."

"Oh, I got you another present as well as this little one," says James, grinning at me and tapping Alfie on the shoulder.

"Oh, yeah. Yeah. That's right. I've got important things to do right now," says Alfie theatrically, backing out of the room. He scampers up the stairs.

I take the little gift from James and carefully peel off the wrapping paper, revealing a red velvet box. Even though I have an idea what's inside, tears well in my eyes. I open the box, but the solitaire diamond ring is all blurry in my swimming vision.

"Flo Simmons," James says softly, taking my hand in his. "You have brought so much joy into my life. I love you more than words can express." He takes the ring from its box and drops to one knee. I feel like a princess. James is my prince. "Please, please marry me."

"I absolutely adore you, James Hadley. I'd love to be your wife." James slips the ring onto my finger, then stands and looks deep into my eyes. He brushes the happy tears from my cheeks. Then he kisses me, sweetly, like the first time we kissed on the silent snowy street.

"Did she say yes, Dad?" yells Alfie from the doorway. "Are you going to be my new mom, Miss Simmons? I mean, Flo?"

**The End**

I hope you enjoyed Flo and James's story!

Don't miss out on the rest of the ***Letter to Mrs. Claus*** Series!

You can find all twelve standalone, kisses-only holiday romcoms on ***Amazon***.

*A Mistletoe Mix Up by Belle Greene*

*A Not So Merry Kiss-mas by Abby Greyson*

*A Christmas Court(ship) by Tiffany Noelle Chacon*

*Cozy by the Fire(man) by Lindsay Rochester*

*The Christmas Reboot by Leah Busboom*

*The Letters We Don't Expect by Evie Sterling*

*Finding You This Christmas by Hazel Belle*

*Lighting Up My Christmas by Cindy Ray Hale*

*Chloe Foster's Holiday Rewrite by Britney M. Mills*

*Nicked by the Mistletoe by Ellie Hartwood*

*Matched With My Christmas Crush by Francesca Spencer*

*Christmas Wishes & Accountant Kisses by Madelyn Smith*

To read the rest of the *Letters to Mrs. Claus* series, scan the QR code with the camera on your phone then click the link.

If you would like to read another one of Francesca Spencer's heartwarming tales, you can find the first chapter of **Stuck With My Christmas Crush** on the next page.

Enjoy!

# Stuck With My Christmas Crush

## AWARD-WINNING ROMCOM

**SWEET CHRISTMAS KISSES SERIES**

*Stuck* WITH MY *Christmas Crush*

FRANCESCA SPENCER

## CHAPTER 1

### Jason

"Come on, Maddie. We don't want to keep your mom waiting." I open the car door and stand aside as my niece climbs into the back seat of my Chevy. "Remember to buckle up."

"Of course, Jason. You treat me like a child."

"You're six years old, Maddie. You qualify."

She huffs at me as I check her seatbelt and then carefully shut the door.

"Rocko." My dog, a mastiff cross, lifts his floppy ears and tilts his head. He listens, alert and attentive. "Be on guard til I get back, okay?" I check the time on my Fitbit. "Between fourteen-thirty and fifteen hundred hours."

"He really understands, doesn't he?" says Maddie, more of a statement than a question, as I get into the driver's seat and start the engine.

"Yup. He's a very smart dog." I turn around to face Maddie. "All set? You got everything?"

"I think so."

"Let's go."

I shift the truck into gear and drive slowly through the open gate. The engine chugs as I slip into neutral, pull on the handbrake and get out to shut the gate behind me. I pull the hefty chain through the impressive wrought iron gates, but I don't bother securing the padlock. From the road, the gates look shut and locked, and with Rocko on patrol, there's little chance of an intruder chancing his luck.

"Good boy." My dog sits patiently behind the gate as I get back into my truck. I watch him in the rearview as I make a final adjustment to the mirror. His eyes don't lose focus as I drive to the road. He's still in the same spot when I make the turn in the direction of the main highway.

"Did you have fun today?" I flick a glance at Maddie who is looking out of the window. She's bundled up in her cute pink woolly hat and padded jacket.

"Yes, Jason. Thanks for asking. Rocko and I had a lovely time."

"That's good. I'm glad. It's always a pleasure to have your company, Maddie."

My niece has started talking in a way that she thinks sounds like a princess since I moved into the Mansion Hotel. Maddie loves the ramshackle, dilapidated, moldering pile. Me, not so much.

I'm only there for a short time, living in the tiny gatehouse on the once-grand estate. The situation is not ideal. And, to be honest, inheriting a property like this one is a massive headache. But, I signed the papers and now I'm the proud owner of a serious money pit. Bills started rolling in even before the ink dried at the lawyer's office, making my head spin, my bank account set to freefall, and my stomach tie itself in anxiety knots. Conveniently, I'm in between contracts at the present time. I told my agent to hold off putting me forward for anything until after the holidays. So, here I am, overseeing the inventory and imminent sale of the land, buildings, and chattels therein. I can't wait to flick it off and move on to my next engineering job, wherever that may be. Until such times, and because there needs to be someone onsite for security reasons, it just seemed obvious that I would move in. Temporarily. Just until things get sorted out, or until I get some kind of security system installed. I want to be free of this burden and get my life back. The sooner the better.

"Can you play some Christmas music?"

"Really?"

"Yes. We can sing along."

"Maddie. I'd really rather not."

"Jason. Don't be such a Grinch."

"I'm not a Grinch. I just don't want jingle bells when I'm driving... It's distracting."

"Fine. But, you know, you're heading for the naughty list, and you won't get any presents."

Maddie sees me looking at her in the rearview and huffs. She looks out of the window again, her hands clasped in her lap like the portrait of the lady in the Mansion Hotel's grand entrance hall.

My niece is adorable, although demanding. She melts my heart, and I love my role as uncle, although Maddie just calls me Jason, without the label.

"Look, Jason. There's a fairy driving a ladybug," says Maddie as I drive past a red VW at the side of the road which has been painted with black dots. The car is stationary. Its hazard lights are on. "Hey. I think it's the same fairy who came to Isabel's party."

"Maddie. Do you think there might be more than one fairy?" I can't believe what I just said. I laugh to myself, bite my lip, and roll my eyes.

"Well, duh. Of course, there's more than one fairy. I can name them for you, if you want."

"No, that's okay." I slow down and indicate a U-turn. "The fairy looks like she needs some help. Let's go ask?"

"Sure."

The road from the mansion links up to the main highway north and south, but it's windy and narrow and, unless you live up here, there's no advantage to using this route. The lack of traffic means that the road is not well-maintained and takes you up and over a hill instead of around it. I hardly ever see another vehicle when I'm driving to or from Ridgewood, the nearest town, about an hour away.

As I approach the ladybug car, the fairy lowers her phone and pulls the light-colored faux fur jacket tightly around her shoulders. She eyes me suspiciously as I park the Chevy close by in front of her.

"Hey there," I say, getting out and beginning to walk toward the young woman all decked out in glittery pink. "We noticed your hazards are on. Is everything alright?"

"Hi there. Thanks for stopping. Bertie's broken down. But I called the roadside assistance." The fairy holds up her phone as if showing me proof of her actions. "They should be here soon," she says with a nervous smile.

"It might be something simple like a dead battery," I offer. "Do you have jumper cables? I have some in the truck." I turn to point over my shoulder, then notice Maddie is at my side.

"Excuse me, fairy," says Maddie in her most polite princess voice. "Were you at my friend, Isabel's party in the summertime?"

The fairy seems to relax at the sight of a little girl and gets out of her car.

"Isabel. Mmmm. Let me see." The fairy considers Maddie's question. "Was that the party at a big white house? Does your friend have a naughty cat called Custard who tried to jump onto the table to eat the cake?"

"That's right!" says Maddie, delighted. She turns to me and beams a bright smile. "It is her. See, I told you."

"Maddie is seldom wrong." I reach out to stroke Maddie's hair. She leans casually onto my leg.

"Don't you remember?" Maddie says, looking up at me.

I glance from Maddie to the glittery girl and see something familiar in her eyes. A fleeting memory flashes of the warm summer's day when I picked Maddie up from her friend's party. As I arrived on the street outside Maddie's friend's house, a van pulled away and, for a second, I was caught in the gaze of an incredibly pretty woman; the same pretty woman who is standing beside the broken red, black-spotted, ladybug car.

"No. Sorry Maddie, I don't," I lie, but the fairy looks at me and recognition lights up her face.

She's about to say something. Her pretty lips open, then, in an instant, she checks herself, and they close again. A hand covers her mouth.

I'm conscious that I may be staring but I'm mesmerized by her face which is decorated with swirls and daubs of glittery paint. Her clear blue eyes sparkle more than the sequins on her dress.

To distract myself, I clear my throat with a cough then say, "So, do you want to get a jumpstart? Or maybe you might be out of gas, in which case, I can tow you to a gas station?"

"That's kind of you, sir," the fairy says looking directly into my eyes. "But don't let me hold you up. A trained professional is on their way." The fairy checks her phone. "They'll be here in a few minutes. At least, that's what the guy said." She laughs. "Thanks anyway."

"If you are sure you're okay," I say as Maddie reaches up and takes my hand. "Then, we'll be off."

"No," says Maddie emphatically stamping her foot. "We can't leave her here."

"Don't worry Maddie." The fairy crouches down, smiles at my niece, and whispers, "I have special magic, so I'll be okay."

Maddie thinks for a moment, then says, "If you have special magic, then you should use it to fix your car."

"Good point. And I would if I could but sadly, my poor car, Bertie, has been cursed by an evil wizard, and the only way the curse can be lifted is by a roadside assistance technician wizard." The fairy stands up and pats the hood of the little VW. Then she looks at me and says, "I'm fine. Really. But thanks, again, for stopping." She turns to climb into her car but pauses to wave and says, "Bye Maddie. Say hi to Isabel and Custard when you see them again, okay?"

"Okay, I will," Maddie says back. "Nice to see you again fairy Charlie."

"Charlie?"

"Yup. Fairy Charlie. That's me." The fairy smiles and, pulling the jacket tighter around her, she says, "And Merry Christmas."

"Alright." I stand still for an awkward moment, glancing up and then down, the road as I decide what to do. "We should get going. Maddie go get in the car. And make sure you..." Maddie finishes my sentence.

"Buckle up. I know."

Part of me wants to stay until the roadside recovery people arrive, but I promised Meredith that Maddie would be home by now. I check my Fitbit. I'll need to call my sister to say we're going to be late. I'm about to offer Charlie a ride to wherever she needs to be, but her phone rings.

"I'd better get this," she says, stepping into her car. "Thanks again." She closes the door and waves at me through the windshield.

Reluctantly, I drive away.

To keep reading **Stuck With My Christmas Crush,** scan the QR code with the camera on your phone then click the link.

Stuck With My Christmas Crush

**Scan here**

# Thank you!

A huge thank you to you for reading ***Matched With My Christmas Crush.*** If you loved my fun rom-com, then please tell all your friends and leave some kind thoughts and a swag of stars on ***Amazon*** and/or anywhere online.

Loads of love goes out to my fabulous ARC team, my family and, of course, Chloe, the toothless Chihuahua.

I couldn't do any of this writing malarky without the love and support of friends, family, and, of course, readers!

So, let's stay in touch.

Find me on Facebook or Instagram. Or download ***Mr Off-limits Grump*** from my website - a little gift for lovely readers who join my mailing list. Look out for another special surprise gift when you sign up.

Writers need readers, so thank you!

Thank you to the other authors in the fabulous *Letters to Mrs Claus* series for a wonderful collaborative experience.

You will always have a special glowing festive ember in my heart.

Special thanks and love go out to Dorothy, my brilliant mum. I am forever grateful.

More soon.

x

*Francesca Spencer*

Laughs, Heart and Happily Ever After

**www.francescaspencerauthor.com**

Printed in Dunstable, United Kingdom